A GENTLEMAN'S DAUGHTER

SISTERS

of the

REVOLUTION #1

Diana Davis

DCB

DAUGHTERS OF COLUMBIA BOOKS

A GENTLEMAN'S DAUGHTER © 2020 Diana Davis

First printing, 2020

Published by Daughters of Columbia Books

ISBN 978-1-940096-41-4

PRINTED IN THE UNITED STATES OF AMERICA

A
GENTLEMAN'S
DAUGHTER

—For L.D.B.
You are an inspiration

Chapter 1

*C*assandra Crofton had never been to a dock before, but as she stepped out of the coach after her sister, she was instantly certain she did not like them. Between the stench and the noise, clearly this was no place for a gentleman's daughters, no matter how far they were being forced to travel.

The familiar ache returned to her heart. The time had come. They were leaving England.

Lowell, their villainous cousin, approached a sailor. "This is the *Rimington*, correct? Bound for the colonies?"

"Philadelphia, that's the one."

Cassandra stared up at the vessel, covered in a web of its own rigging. The paint peeling off the sides gave it a haunted appearance. Surely this ship could not safely carry them for the six-week voyage across an ocean—and that time estimate was if conditions were favorable.

"I've purchased passage for these two." Cousin Lowell pointed at Cassandra and her older sister, Helen.

"Women?" The sailor squinted at them, as if he couldn't tell their gender from their appearance.

"Ladies," Cassandra corrected him.

The sailor turned back to Lowell. "Jest these two? Without you?"

"Yes. They have one another for chaperones."

Cassandra pressed her lips together to hold back an impertinent remark. While traveling together saved them a small shred of dignity, this was clearly not the way things were done in their society.

Lowell didn't look at them as he paid the sailor and directed him toward their waiting trunks. To be sure, Lowell was glad to be rid of them at last. The letter from Uncle Josiah accepting their charge had arrived less than a fortnight ago, and Lowell had immediately made the arrangements final.

Two sailors fetched their trunks, hauling them up the gangway.

Cassandra studied the ship in front of them, her stomach already rolling as if they were onboard. She glanced over at Helen, but she did not find reassurance. Instead, she found resolve in looking at her sister's riding habit, dyed black like her own.

Suddenly moving to the American colonies still felt incredibly unwise, but they no longer had an alternative. They had to get across this ocean to the only family that would have them.

Cassandra looked back to bid Lowell farewell. He was perhaps the one part of England she would never miss. However, he had already boarded the coach and shut the door.

Very well, then. She and Helen turned to each other, her sister offering an encouraging smile. "It will be an adventure," Helen said. Her eyes said her words were an effort to convince herself as much as Cassandra.

"Yes." Cassandra hoped her voice held more conviction,

but she doubted it.

Little else remained between them and their fate: leaving England, most likely forever.

By unspoken signal, Cassandra and Helen clasped hands. They'd already said their goodbyes in Surrey. No one else was at the docks to see them off.

"Ready?" Helen asked.

Yes. It was time. Time to be brave. Every feeling in her chest seemed to cry out that this was wrong, but Cassandra took a bracing breath and tamped down her emotions. She moved forward, and so did Helen.

Before Cassandra made it two steps, however, a tall man in an impeccable wig and fine coat of green velvet strolled past them, cutting off their path. Behind him trailed a short, portly servant. The nobleman paused, allowing the servant to trot ahead to the ship's crew.

Helen cast a sly look at Cassandra. They had had enough of society for Cassandra to know immediately what her sister meant. While a man that handsome and obviously rich would have had every eligible girl in Surrey vying for a dance, this popinjay was sorely out of place on the docks.

He had yet to notice—or care—that he had cut them off. Helen rerouted around him and Cassandra followed her. Honestly, Cassandra might never understand how the nobility could be so blessedly ignorant of anyone but themselves at times.

Cassandra gathered her courage again, and she and Helen approached the gangway. For Cassandra's part, she was striving to stride forward and not turn back. They were going to make the best of their reduced situation. At least they would if Uncle Josiah proved as generous as he seemed in his letter.

Taking them in at all was generous. They might have to be grateful he fed them. It was more than Lowell was willing to do now.

But first, they had to get across this ocean.

As they reached the base of the gangway, however, the nobleman's servant held up a hand to stop them. "Pardon me, ladies. One moment."

Cassandra and Helen halted abruptly. Would that same nobleman hold them up a second time? Were they supposed to observe precedence in boarding a ship?

Apparently so. The nobleman finally deigned to approach, staring down his Roman nose at them. His expression could best be described as a simper, but noblemen surely did not simper.

He did not bother to address them, as if they were so beneath his notice, he had no need of acknowledging their existence.

Had they been at Heartcomb, he would have given their father his respect. He would have wanted to know their names. He would have danced with them, were he lucky enough to find them unengaged.

Instead, he saw them as less than the sailors hauling his trunks up the gangway for him.

"Why on earth would such a nobleman travel to the Americas?" Helen murmured. They both glanced at the servant, but he didn't seem to have heard them. He paid a crew member and marched back to his coach.

The sailor gestured for them to pass, and Helen and Cassandra nodded their thanks. At least they had been taught how to treat people beneath them. There was no excuse for such ill-breeding.

On deck, the rocking of the boat, even anchored, was not the only reason Cassandra felt unsettled. The crew seemed to watch them with suspicion. Surely there were other women making this voyage. They could be the only ones making the journey alone, however.

Or perhaps it was their attire. Their habits and hats had to betray their class. Yes, moving across an ocean was hardly a thing ladies of good breeding did—unless they had been orphaned and impoverished.

Perhaps the clothing on his back—and the contents of his multitude of trunks, still making their way up the gangway— were the popinjay's last possessions left in the world. His wig might have been freshly powdered and his valet might have just taken care of his business, but if he were that well off, why would he be making such a journey? They weren't crossing an ocean willingly, that was certain.

A throat cleared next to Cassandra and she turned. There stood the nobleman in question, and at a closer range, she saw the fine detailing of the gold braid along his coat. Perhaps he was not quite so reduced in circumstances as she'd imagined.

The nobleman pointed at her, then flicked his wrist, as if he were too good to use words to command her to move. Cassandra checked behind her. A carrier bearing yet another heavy trunk stood behind her, waiting to pass.

"Pardon me," Cassandra said, quickly sweeping out of his path.

The coxcomb practically snorted. "I should think so."

Cassandra glared at him with such heat he should have withered. Helen took her arm, as if cautioning her from unleashing her tongue.

Instead, Helen did the honors. "Dearest, do you remember what they said at Heartcomb about men in ditto suits?" Although Helen clearly addressed Cassandra, no one could be ignorant that she referred to the popinjay's matching coat, waistcoat and breeches.

"Oh, yes. They haven't the imagination to coordinate any other *ensemble*."

The nobleman laughed, a single syllable entirely through his nose. "How very low."

Before Cassandra or Helen could defend themselves, the coxcomb strutted away.

Both of them turned away in disgust, approaching the ship's railing. "What a peacock," Helen muttered.

"Practically a macaroni." That was not strictly true; he was fashionable without becoming a caricature.

"Exactly how one should outfit one's self for a voyage overseas of at least six weeks."

Their own dark grey riding habits, formerly navy and red, were much more hardwearing than such finery. Still, with their own complements of braid and buttons, Cassandra did not think they were so poorly turned out to merit such disdain.

On the other hand, perhaps she should be grateful for the popinjay's distraction from her pain. The view from the ship's railing held only the dock they'd just left. While it was far from Cassandra's most beloved part of England, in both the geographic and metaphoric senses, she still couldn't bear to stare at it. She turned away before tears could threaten.

Her sister seemed to agree. "Let's find someone to help us to our quarters," Helen suggested. "Hopefully we shan't have to deal with *him* much on the voyage."

"Or in the colonies." With any luck, Philadelphia would not be his final destination.

Helen located a seaman who did not appear to be overly busy sunning himself, and he obliged them by leading them below deck, the ladies grasping onto railings and walls the whole way.

If Cassandra had been put off by the exterior of the ship, the interior was even more dispiriting. Although the sun streamed down the stairs after them, the corridor was dark and dank. They were to spend how long in these cramped quarters?

"Only got free cabins fer passengers," the seaman informed them, pointing at each in turn. Cassandra took a moment to infer that "free" referred to the number—three—rather than the status or price of the passage. "Can't say which is yers."

"Thank you," Helen said. "We'll find out."

The seaman gave a mock salute and headed away. Cassandra and Helen each peered into a room. Upon her opening the door, the bright light through the window blinded Cassandra for a moment.

"I beg your pardon!" The green velvet popinjay scowled at Cassandra from inside the cabin.

"My apologies." She hurried to step back. How had the nobleman gotten down here ahead of them?

The popinjay stalked to the door. "I don't know how you people behave where you come from," he sneered, "but while we are aboard this vessel, I shall thank you not to barge into my chambers."

Cassandra found herself unusually thunderstruck. The first reflexive defense her mind mustered was to drop into a slight curtsy.

Precisely the fuel this nobleman would need to seal his judgment of her, to be sure.

"Dearest." Helen appeared at her elbow. "I found our quarters." She scrutinized the coxcomb up and down. "What have you found?"

At last, Cassandra recovered. "Someone whose rank is far above his breeding, it appears."

The nobleman's eyes flashed. Her comment had found its mark. He gaped at her a moment, then snapped his mouth shut. Whether he thought himself too good to respond or simply couldn't think of an answer, she couldn't say.

Cassandra looped her arm in Helen's, and they strode off

to their own cramped quarters, less than half the size of the nobleman's.

Helen launched into her lecture the moment they were alone. "It won't do to make enemies before we've left English soil."

Cassandra peered out the round window at the water outside. "But we've already left English soil."

She looked at her sister, their eyes finally filling with tears.

Helen recovered first, drawing a breath and swiping at her cheeks. "The colonies will be wonderful," she said. "I'm sure they're not as bad as everyone says."

"Uncle Josiah wouldn't have stayed if they were. Unless he couldn't stand to make the return voyage." Cassandra pressed a hand to her queasy stomach. Perhaps sitting would help. She scanned the room, bare but for two bunks and two trunks. She wanted to lie in the bunk and not get up ever, especially not in the colonies, but she settled on her trunk.

Helen's quiet sobs filled the room again. Cassandra put aside her own pain. She could do this one small thing for her sister. "Uncle Josiah must be very kind, mustn't he?"

"He *is* taking us in." Helen steadied herself against the window's round frame and drew a shaking breath.

"If he's anything like Mama, he'll be the kindest man in all of Pennsylvania," Cassandra tried once more.

Helen managed a weak smile. "He left a very long time ago."

Cassandra knew the story well: not long before she and Helen were born, Mama's brothers, Josiah and William, set off for the colonies in search of adventure and glory in King George's War. Instead, Josiah had met a wife—a Quaker woman, if the family rumor were true—and William had met his end.

Cassandra looked to Helen. She couldn't be sure whether

her sister was quite so pale because of the ship's gentle bobbing or because she was thinking of Uncle William's untimely death.

Surely the colonies couldn't be that dangerous, could they? "We shall be perfectly fine," Cassandra promised her sister. "We only have to get to Uncle Josiah."

"Perhaps the voyage won't be quite so dreadful," Helen said, making her tottering way to her own trunk. "We've already made a new friend."

Cassandra laughed at both the joke and from relief that Helen's spirits were buoyed. But her sister was right. The next six weeks—or more—would only be tolerable if they could stay far away from that popinjay.

Chapter 2

The Lord David Beaufort set the tin plate of hard tack biscuits aside on one of his trunks of books. He had never before made such a terrible mistake, and he didn't just mean the food.

He laid back on his hard bunk. He'd sensed it from the moment he'd boarded this dreadful little dinghy, and four weeks at sea had done little to change his mind. At the outset they'd hoped to make the journey in six weeks, but the captain had informed him that two storms and low wind had set them at least ten days behind that schedule.

As much as he wanted off this ship, part of him was looking forward to his task in Philadelphia even less. He had finally become accustomed to the constant rolling of the waves, after spending far too much time above deck below the weather and losing his second-best wig overboard along with what passed for a meal here. He glanced at the hard tack he couldn't choke down today. Small wonder half the sailors had but half their teeth if this was their diet.

Lord David spent as little time in his stifling cabin as he

could, but the alternative was milling around in the hold with the ship's other passengers who were so very common. Their manners and dress and ... aroma turned his stomach almost as much as the ship's motion had.

So above deck it was. He climbed out of his bunk and ascended topside. Passengers were not actually welcome on deck—he could tell he got in the working sailors' way from time to time—and he hardly wanted to spend more time in the sun, but at least he could find air up here. The breeze was pleasant.

He strode across the deck. Clearly he would never develop the sea legs of the sailors, but at last he felt more at ease on the boat. The horizon held nothing but the open ocean in every direction, their ship a tiny speck in a vast, literal sea.

How was this going to prove his quality?

Knowing his parents, how would anything?

"Pardon," a sailor pushing a mop muttered.

Lord David stepped back from this sortie. The only people to which he might have possibly spoken were the captain, who was obviously busy, and still rather beneath him, and the occupants of the other two cabins. Unfortunately, as he outranked them, he would have had to give assent, and they had no acquaintance to introduce them.

He had deduced that the couple in one cabin and the pair of sisters in the other were not completely destitute. The couple were apparently merchants hoping to establish a shop in the colonies. He could only assume from the somber colors of their attire that the sisters were either hopeless in fashion or mourning a close relative. Both seemed equally probable after their attempt at ridiculing his own apparel.

It was likely better this way. He'd spent enough of his life being disrespected; he wasn't about to let someone else treat him that way. Nothing was to be gained from associating with them, and he was not quite so desperate for company that he needed to lower himself that much.

Yet.

Though he'd never inherit his father's title, he had learned long ago that his rank often meant that he would be alone. No reason to believe that would change now, not aboard this ship and not once they reached the colonies.

What was he thinking? Young men of rank did not run away to America to build their own fortunes. No matter how little they had to do with their family's estate, no matter how little consequence they had in their own lives, no matter how much they wished to ... matter.

Lord David paced to the other side of the ship. The other side of the ocean held nothing for him either.

He could buy passage back as soon as they landed. On this very ship, or perhaps something nicer, departing sooner. In another three months, he could be back in silly Somerset society, courting the same silly society girls at the same silly society suppers and balls.

He could have lived his entire life there. He could have done exactly what everyone expected of him. He could have slipped into the background of every conversation and every ball and every life, as he'd been forced to from birth.

Lord David strode back to his first position. He'd made this choice for a reason. He could wait a few weeks before he made any rash decisions.

High, light laughter carried to his ears and for a moment, he did fancy himself back in Somerset society. He turned and found the sisters, each swathed in fashionably cut grey silk.

They were handsome women; he could give them that. Even if he hadn't heard they were sisters, they favored one another so strongly he would have guessed it. He'd gathered the elder was the slightly taller one and the one with narrower features the younger, though they both had to be above twenty, which would put them within a few years of himself.

Lord David pivoted away. The sisters did not belong above deck, and to be sure, they did not belong in his company either. He wasn't about to forget his place simply because it had been his place to be forgotten.

Furthermore, the sisters had little sense of propriety, sailing off to the colonies unaccompanied. They had attempted to insult him multiple times upon their first meeting. He'd successfully avoided them almost all of the time since, so they hadn't repeated the offense, but he didn't mean to give them the opportunity, either.

The laughter drew closer. Lord David clasped his hands behind his back and began to stroll away. The mopping sailor, however, cut off his route, forcing Lord David back to the sisters. They were terribly close. Now he could not turn away without obviously snubbing them. They were hardly the sort of society that would merit such a stroke.

The mopping sailor conspired against him again a moment later as he mopped right past the women. The motion combined with a swell set the younger sister off balance. She tottered for a moment before she teetered backward—toward him.

At the last moment, David caught her before she crashed into him. "I beg your pardon," he said. He was fairly certain it had become the phrase he'd used the most with the other passengers, in various shades of apology or indignation.

The sister righted herself. "It's no matter."

It was no matter? That time was not an apology. "Excuse me, is it possible you do not know who I am?"

"Obviously I do not." She smiled, but it was the look of someone who had ensnared her quarry. "As we have never been introduced."

14

Lord David opened his mouth but immediately thought better of it. What was he to do, lower himself and introduce himself like a commoner?

The older sister took the other's arm, but the younger woman arched an eyebrow. "Ah, then you do not know who you are either?"

Yes, this was exactly why he had avoided them. "Perhaps," he said, pouring as much ice into his tone as would fit in his father's icehouse, "I do not wish to make your acquaintance."

"That has been completely clear," the younger sister snapped. "And it suits perfectly. I'll happily persist in not knowing you if making your acquaintance would require a gentleman's daughter to bow and scrape to someone of so little consequence. Good day."

Neither woman showed any sign of remorse for that level of effrontery. Neither of them made any move at all, forcing Lord David to give a curt bow and stride away.

A gentleman's daughter? How very likely. Certainly not any sort of gentleman he'd ever known. He wasn't about to throw his father's title around, and he was a marquess.

This was exactly the sort of silly society he wanted to escape. Yes, he should be accorded the respect commensurate with his rank, but all the ridiculousness of the self-important, immodest imbeciles—

Lord David schooled his thoughts with a deep breath. As ill-advised as this voyage seemed at times, he had to remember its purpose. He wished to distance himself from the vainglorious, simpering society he'd always associated with, and to do something of consequence.

And that was the real reason why the younger sister's words hurt.

There, he had admitted it: she'd injured him. She was of no consequence herself, but her words had found their mark.

Again.

The sooner they reached their destination and he was out of close quarters with that woman, the better.

Cassandra finished a sweep of their empty cabin and locked her trunk for the final time. The forecast of six weeks at sea, as it happened, was overly optimistic. In all, the nine weeks of their voyage passed with agonizing slowness. Cassandra and Helen had befriended the merchant and his wife occupying the other cabin, as well as a few of the lower sort of passengers, but they soon ran out of things to discuss. The sailors were busy working, and not much in the art of conversation in the first place. Probably why they'd taken to the sea.

Cassandra could own it: she'd felt like she'd nearly lost her mind trapped on this ship. She'd already read all the books both she and Helen had brought—not many, as they'd hoped they'd be able to find more in Philadelphia. It couldn't be *that* backward, could it?

That nobleman had to have an entire trunk full of books among the nine she'd counted as he'd boarded, and there could well be more. Or perhaps they were all full of clothes.

It didn't matter. They would get shut of him now that they had reached the colonies.

Cassandra tidied their cabin for the final time, making sure they had left nothing unpacked. Their meager trunks were filled and ready to find their way to Uncle Josiah's. To their new home.

"Are you ready?" Helen asked.

Cassandra looked at their trunks. Nothing compared to

what the coxcomb had brought. "Yes," Cassandra replied. She followed Helen through the narrow corridor that felt so familiar it was their home now, up to the deck. She pulled the back of her neckerchief higher to protect her skin from the sun, her better straw hat already carefully packed away.

When they reached the railing, the first inescapable sight was not the city. It was the *twelve* trunks piled on the deck to disembark, all bearing the same coat of arms.

"Twelve?" Cassandra breathed, counting again.

Helen shook her head in wonder. "That man could have bought Heartcomb and never missed the money. We could have at least stayed on as tenants."

That much wealth was almost unseemly, even to Cassandra. However, they'd well learned that no amount of money could make up for ill breeding. "Yes, but he would be every bit as disagreeable as Cousin Lowell."

Helen had to agree with that assessment. Cassandra finally moved past the trunks, both physically and metaphorically, as she stepped to the ship's railing. Helen joined her for their first look at Philadelphia.

It was not as quaint as she had expected. In fact, the civilization of the tall brick buildings almost seemed to rival London, as rare as their visits there had been. Cassandra glanced at Helen. She, too, seemed pleasantly surprised.

"Do you see Uncle Josiah?" Cassandra asked, although neither of them had any idea what he might look like.

Helen scanned the crowd. "I don't know." She took her sister's hand. They would find him.

A man began shouting behind them, and they both turned to see what was the matter. The popinjay was there behind them, and for a brief second, Cassandra assumed that he had caused the fuss, probably demanding to be treated as befitting his rank, which had to be some lowly baronet or other. He had put on a fine white wig over his dark hair for the first time in weeks, but he could scarcely be older than them.

However, once she craned her neck to see past him, Cassandra found that it was a sailor clamoring. The commoner passengers were being herded onto the deck.

"What's happening?" Cassandra murmured to Helen.

"I don't know," the nobleman replied from her other side. Something in his aggravatingly handsome face was watchful of the growing commotion on the deck.

She was most definitely not addressing him, but decided the matter was not worth pursuing. Furthermore, he wasn't *that* handsome.

The ranking seaman selected several of the male passengers from the crowd and commissioned them to help carry the coxcomb's trunks.

"Is this what it means to be a servant in the Americas?" the nobleman murmured.

Cassandra couldn't read his tone, but he did not seem entirely pleased, although his trunks were already making their way down the gangway. "What? Are they not bowing and scraping deeply enough, Your Highness?"

He turned a cool look on her. "Where I come from, we hire servants. We don't press people off the street."

Cassandra could only manage a quizzical expression. His Highness the Popinjay . . . cared about commoners?

Before she could understand what that might mean, the nobleman strode away, down the gangway.

"That's the last we'll see of him," Helen said. "And good riddance."

"Indeed." While Cassandra agreed, she would have done so more emphatically five minutes ago.

"All right," the captain said, waving them toward the gangway. "All off."

Helen and Cassandra headed down the gangway, the rest of the passengers following them. On the docks, Cassandra discovered that America was much less *terra firma* than England. Why did the land feel so much less steady than the boat had? The captain guffawed at her tottering steps. "You'll find your land legs again; give it time."

"Thank you," she managed. Helen fished Uncle Josiah's letter from her pocket while Cassandra found their trunks, piled among The Lord High Popinjay's things.

His Lordship watched, arms folded, as Helen instructed a dock worker to transport their things to Josiah Hayes in Society Hill, but neither of them could describe his house. This didn't trouble the dock worker, who took a whole shilling for the job.

"Don't touch the other trunks," the popinjay commanded.

The dock worker nodded, but his air held less subservience than Cassandra expected.

Perhaps they would like the colonies if it put people like His Worship in his place. The sooner, the better.

"Arright, you girls." A seaman cut between them and the nobleman, herding Helen and Cassandra back with the other passengers.

"What? What's happening?" Helen demanded.

They were brought to stand before the captain, who held out a hand. "Now you pay yer fare."

Cassandra and Helen looked at one another. "What fare?" Helen asked.

"The rest of yer passage."

"There must be some mistake," Helen insisted. "We saw our cousin pay your sailor at the docks. Lowell. Remember?"

The captain checked with his nearest crew members, who each shook their heads. "No one else remembers that, girlies."

He waited for some answer, but they had none. Did he want money? They had only a few pounds to their names.

"We're waiting for our Uncle Josiah," Helen said. "He is to meet us here."

The captain squinted at them, as if too many weeks at sea had dulled his eyesight. "Yer passage wasn't paid free and clear. Off to the market wit' ye."

Market? What would they buy? "No, no, no," Cassandra said. "Then our uncle should never find us."

"If yer not paying, then nobody's meeting anybody here. You're to be indentures."

What? The word seemed to steal Cassandra's breath. They were to be sold as bound labor?

The captain could only offer an open-handed shrug. "Sorry, girls, my hands is tied."

No, they clearly weren't—but Cassandra's and Helen's would be soon. Cassandra scanned the dock for anyone to appeal to, anyone who could help.

The popinjay. She certainly didn't deserve anything from him, but he was the only person there who might be able to compel the captain's compliance. Cassandra locked eyes on him.

He gave her a slow, easy smile, and then a little bow from the neck, as if taking his leave of her.

He was going to let them be carted away to be sold like cattle?

Tears pricked Cassandra's eyes, and she grasped for Helen's hand.

How would Uncle Josiah ever find them now?

Chapter 3

The captain had cleared away the rabble and the impertinent sisters, and Lord David had taken his leave. He'd known, all along, they weren't his sort. Gentleman's daughters indeed. No uncle was coming for them. Obviously he was a ruse invented to get themselves out of the contract they'd agreed to when they'd purchased a cabin but not passage.

Lord David was not about to become another pawn in that scheme.

Now he could set about setting his things to order. He would still have to find a place to stay, but surely a tavern in town would do for now.

"Excuse me," a man said behind him. Lord David turned to find a moderately well dressed man of about fifty addressing him, his dark hair straight and loose.

"Yes?" Lord David kept his tone brusque.

"Is this the *Rimington?*" He pointed at the ship behind them.

David gestured to the side of the ship where its name was

painted. It was the *Rimington*, but he had better things to do.

The man addressed one of the workers helping with Lord David's trunks. "Are there passengers still aboard? I'm trying to find my nieces, Helen and Cassandra Crofton."

Lord David's heart fell an inch. For a moment, he'd allowed himself to believe all the uncharitable thoughts he'd had about the sisters. Even the panic in the younger sister's sweet brown eyes he'd believed feigned.

Had the sister given her uncle's name? He turned to address the colonist. "Josiah Hayes?"

The man cocked his head slightly. "You have the advantage of me, sir."

No alternative this time. He gave a curt neck bow. "Lord David Beaufort."

"Pleasure," Hayes responded, the barest minimum of decency. "Do you know of my nieces?"

"They have been taken to the market to be sold as indentured servants." He pointed in the direction they'd been taken.

Hayes drew a sharp breath. "Thank you, Lord Beaufort. Please, do call on us in Society Hill so I may thank you properly."

Lord David gave another neck bow to dismiss the effusive man. He was not properly addressed as Lord Beaufort, but that was no matter. Josiah Hayes hurried off to rescue his nieces.

Something about the man stayed with Lord David as he coped with his affairs, including the two extra trunks that apparently he would have to get to Society Hill now. That man cared that much about his nieces? Lord David couldn't even tell if they'd ever met.

Well, for his part, he hoped Josiah Hayes found his nieces. Helen and Cassandra Crofton. Lord David pushed the names out of his mind. He would never see them again. Noting their names was unnecessary.

Where had they come to? Cassandra clung to Helen's hands, watching the impromptu market warily. On the street in front of a coffeehouse, various merchants, tradesmen and farmers inspected them and their fellow passengers as if they were livestock. They were certainly herded together like animals, the market surrounded by chains. The terror in the children's eyes echoed her own.

How was this allowed in a civilized society?

Next to her, a coarse man in coarser clothing haggled with a mother for her daughter, who could not have been more than ten. Everything within Cassandra ached to free the little girl, her siblings, her mother. A year ago, she would have had the means to free them all. Now she shared their fate.

Was this Cousin Lowell's design all along in sending them away? Had he really not paid sufficiently for their passage, or was the captain or crew being unscrupulous? Cassandra was unsure which was worse.

"Crofton!" a rough voice called.

Helen and Cassandra turned. A man in a homespun suit stood next to the captain, who was beckoning them over. The man counted out coins into the captain's other hand.

This couldn't be happening. Surely they would awaken from this nightmare.

Did they have any legal recourse here? If they had some way to find Uncle Josiah, he would surely know.

The man who'd bought them approached. Cassandra could barely breathe. Helen clutched at her hands even tighter. Their new master seemed simple and straightforward, but what kind of person bought another?

The man searched their faces as he got closer. Assessing

them like cattle.

"Helen?" the man said. "Cassandra?"

Cassandra looked to her sister. How did he—?

The man gestured at himself. "Josiah Hayes."

These were not the circumstances they had expected to meet their new guardian under. "Uncle Josiah?" Helen asked.

He glanced around the market, then held out a hand toward the exit. "Shall we?"

Cassandra gave the little girl next to them a final glance. She looked up at them with doleful eyes. Cassandra felt like a villain leaving her, but there was nothing more she could do. They'd just watched Uncle Josiah purchase their own bond. Now she and Helen were indentured servants themselves, bound to the Hayes family for an unknown period of time.

Did they dare discuss the terms of their servitude with Uncle Josiah now? He strode quickly down the wide pebblestone street back toward the docks, and they had to hurry to keep up with him.

Could they not hire a coach? Was that not done in Philadelphia? Were there no coaches for hire in the Americas?

With each step, Cassandra's questions seemed to double. She had spent so much of her worry on simply getting across the ocean that she hadn't spared a thought for what would happen when they arrived. And now they knew: they were to be servants.

They came even with the *Rimington* again, and the popinjay was still marshalling his trunks along with multiple dock workers. "Wait here a moment," Uncle Josiah bade them.

Helen took hold of Cassandra's arm. "Being a maid in Uncle Josiah's house will be leagues better than being a countess in Cousin Lowell's," Helen murmured.

"To be sure." That didn't make it any less difficult to lower themselves so.

Uncle Josiah crossed the street to where the popinjay was inventorying his possessions for the thirtieth time. And then Uncle Josiah approached the coxcomb. And spoke to him. As he might to any other man.

"Am I dreaming?" Cassandra asked.

"Only if we both are," Helen said. "Does he ... *know* that popinjay?"

That would be just the thing, if they'd traveled all this way, uncomfortably edging past one another, and he proved to be some cousin or other.

But the popinjay shook Uncle Josiah's hand. Then the coxcomb pointed out which two trunks were theirs. Had the dock worker simply taken Helen's shilling and absconded?

As if in answer to her question, the popinjay gave Uncle Josiah a coin.

Cassandra and Helen slowly looked at one another. That coxcomb?

Uncle Josiah hurried back across the street to them and showed them to a waiting coach. Helen and Cassandra boarded while Uncle Josiah directed the dock workers who had been handling the popinjay's things to load their trunks onto the coach.

Helen and Cassandra were without words until they were underway. "Uncle," Cassandra finally began, "did you know that nobleman?"

"Oh, no, but he was quite helpful to me."

Yes, they'd seen that. Was this how it was done in the colonies? One simply walked up to nobility and asked them for help?

"Here's your shilling." He handed the coin to Helen. "You had us all worried, taking so long in the crossing. Let me see you," Uncle Josiah said, peering under the brims of their traveling hats. "I see her in you. Elizabeth."

Cassandra beamed, though strictly speaking that was an exaggeration for her part. They both had their father's dark hair, but Cassandra had also inherited his narrower features.

Still, it was a small comfort to hear. At times, she scarcely remembered her mother's face, though it had only been nine years since she'd gone. Mama was only a few years younger than they were now when Uncle Josiah left England.

"Thank you," Helen said for both of them. "Did you know Papa well?"

"Oh yes, we were at school together." Uncle Josiah chuckled. "He was a wit, wasn't he?"

Helen and Cassandra both agreed.

Uncle Josiah's smile grew sympathetic. "I was so sorry to hear of his passing."

"Thank you," Helen said again.

Cassandra knew she should be taking in the city, her first time in this new place, but instead she found herself studying her uncle. There was a certain softness about his features, although he was still perfectly masculine. Something in the shape of his eyes and his smile reminded her of Mama.

The overall effect was to make him seem very kind. Coupled with his neat but plain attire and his choice not to wear a wig, he seemed unassuming. Hopefully he would be a kind master as well.

The ride from the docks to their new home was not terribly far, and soon they were disembarking in front of a small but fashionable house, pink, with multiple stories and a front porch. Uncle Josiah bid his coachman—or perhaps it was a hired cab?—to help with the trunks, and then he himself grabbed a handle.

Unassuming indeed. Cassandra consulted her sister once again, but neither of them knew quite what to make of him.

"Come, girls—rather, ladies," Uncle Josiah bid them. "Meet

your cousins."

They followed him up the steps and into the house. The drawing room was done all in wood paneling, painted a deep green, with an impressive marble fireplace dominating one wall.

"Girls!" Uncle Josiah was calling. "They're here!"

Somewhere above them, a squeal was emitted. A low, approaching rumble began overhead. Cassandra hoped it was more the number of feet doing the stepping, rather than the unladylike behavior of the feet, that produced that much sound.

They had known Uncle Josiah had daughters—that much he had mentioned in his letter—but he hadn't told them very much about their cousins at all.

The room filled with three—no, four—no, *five* young ladies lined up in front of the couch. The oldest seemed to be about Cassandra's age. Their gowns were lovely and well made—if not of the latest English style, a quite recent one.

The oldest, a beauty with hair powdered a shade lighter than theirs, wore a flowered jacket trimmed with fine lace cuffs. She stepped forward, offering her hand. "Good morning! I'm Temperance."

Helen and Cassandra both looked to Uncle Josiah. Would he not introduce them?

"Oh, my apologies, ladies. I've been too long from the mother country. We're prone to introducing ourselves here. Go ahead: it isn't improper." And he left them to make their own introductions.

Helen took Temperance's hand and shook it. "Helen Crofton," she said. Then it was Cassandra's turn, and she gave her name as well. At twenty, Temperance was two years younger than Cassandra and three years younger than Helen.

Next, a quiet girl with piercing eyes and light brown hair,

four years Cassandra's junior. Her gown was a delicate shade of light blue, and her name was Patience.

Constance was next, sixteen, with blonde hair, fine features and rosy cheeks.

Fourth was Verity, with brunette hair and a lovely plump figure in pink stripes.

Last was Mercy, only twelve years old, her blonde ringlets bouncing around her shoulders. She bobbed a little curtsy. "Good morning."

"What a pleasure it is to meet you all," Helen said. Aloud, Cassandra agreed, but her mind was racing, trying to calculate how much time they would have to spend caring for their cousins' hair and wardrobe. Dressing this many mistresses was sure to take them hours.

At least it would be pleasant. All—well, most—of their cousins bore happy and agreeable countenances. Patience would be described more as shrewd, and Mercy as watchful.

Uncle Josiah gestured toward the stairs, where two women descended. "Ladies," he said, addressing Helen and Cassandra, "this is your Aunt Anne."

"How do you do?" they each asked with a curtsy.

Aunt Anne's fine features had the same soft kindness as Uncle Josiah's. She crossed the room to embrace each of them.

Cassandra fought back emotion. It would have been so lovely to be a part of this family, rather than a servant in their home. But she would make the best of the situation presented to her. This was their duty now.

Helen thanked their aunt and uncle again for taking them in, which they quickly dismissed. The second woman still had not warranted an introduction, and a mere glimpse told Cassandra why: her simple, plain jacket and pinned apron showed she was staff in this household.

At least they wouldn't be working alone. Hopefully this

woman could show them the intricacies of their duties.

Uncle Josiah turned to his daughters. "Girls, I'm going back to my office for a while, but I shall return for dinner. Lord David Beaufort will be joining us."

Temperance and Constance exchanged a glance behind Patience's back, excitement flowing between them. Clearly Lord David Beaufort was an important person in their home. The girls' elation definitely seemed to indicate a marriageable man of good standing.

Uncle Josiah bid his wife farewell and left. Constance and Temperance ran to the windows, like girls much younger than twenty and sixteen. Mercy and Verity followed.

"Do you always see your father off this way?" Helen asked Patience, the only cousin remaining with them.

"It's the coach. It's new, and they love to see it and be reminded of how we've attained in status." Her tone was dry, as if such cares were beneath her.

Cassandra watched her cousins. The coach was a symbol of their status? It had been suitable but entirely unremarkable in her estimation.

"Come." Temperance straightened. "We only have two hours to dress for dinner."

Her sisters followed her upstairs in a flutter of petticoats.

If they only had two hours, they had better get to work. Cassandra approached the maid. "Good morning. I'm Cassandra."

The maid consulted Aunt Anne, who merely watched, her face peaceful. "Polly," the maid introduced herself.

Would she have to go by Cassie as a maid? She'd hardly been called that since she was a child. "What shall I do?"

Again, the maid peeked at Aunt Anne. "Go with the girls, naturally."

Of course. Impertinent of her to think she could be trusted

in a kitchen without any training whatsoever when such an important guest was coming. Of all the household duties, ladies' maids would suit them best. They certainly had the most experience with their work, albeit from the receiving end.

"Josiah put your trunks upstairs." Aunt Anne gestured toward the stairs.

Helen and Cassandra both gave a quick little curtsy, as their maids would have done, and hurried upstairs.

"We should get out of these things first," Helen said. She was right, as she usually thought she was. Cassandra followed her, retracing their cousins' path up the stairs and to a large bedroom with three beds.

Mercy, the youngest, hopped off her perch on the bed in the furthest corner. "Papa says you are to have this bed, cousins."

They wouldn't sleep in the staff quarters? "Thank you," Cassandra said. Mercy also pointed out their trunks in the corner.

Her sisters were busily raiding two large wardrobes. With so many daughters, it only made sense to have that many gowns. Cassandra couldn't tell if they were fighting or merely excitedly jabbering, but she was not used to this much commotion to dress, ever.

"Let's hurry," Helen murmured. Cassandra stripped out of her jacket. The military style was almost masculine, and the wool was becoming too warm for the day.

Cassandra dug through her own trunk for the jacket most suitable to a maid. Something plain and hardwearing, most likely. She found a cotton jacket that had been a lovely pink before they'd had it dyed grey for mourning. She matched it with a plain black cotton petticoat.

She pinned her jacket to her stays and tucked in her

neckerchief. Hopefully Polly would have an apron she could use until she could find one herself. She'd done her hair up already this morning, and there wasn't much to be done for that, but she replaced her traveling hat with a frilled cap, her most modest. She would have to try to make it over more simply soon, without the lace and satin ribbon.

Helen finished dressing at the same time, and they turned to one another. A little laugh escaped Helen, and Cassandra had to admit to one as well. Helen's jacket still had lace around the collar and cuffs, and her cap was equally as unsuitable as Cassandra's. They looked ridiculous, as if they were playing at being maids.

But now was not the time for play: it was time for work. They turned to their cousins, all of whom were more or less gaping at them in horror.

Temperance recovered first, venturing over to their corner. "Would you like to borrow a gown?" she asked, holding out the blue floral one she'd taken off.

"Thank you," Helen said, her voice stiff, "but we couldn't possibly."

Constance joined Temperance. "We would love to share." Her smile was so genuine, accentuating her rosy cheeks, that Cassandra felt a tug at her heart. Would they always feel caught between two worlds, living with and serving their cousins?

"Why don't we help you get ready?" Helen's bright tone rang false to Cassandra's ears, but she forced on a happy expression as well.

Temperance and Constance glanced at one another before they accepted slowly. Cassandra chose a lovely pink silk for Temperance, who instantly lit up. "That's my favorite—but I try to save it for special events."

"Like those held at the Governor's Mansion," Patience

said. She had settled in a side chair with a book, apparently not interested in dressing to awe Lord Beaufort.

"How else am I to marry the governor's son?" Temperance trilled back. She turned to Cassandra. "I shall, you know. In time. Papa says I'm still too young."

"Twenty is young," Cassandra agreed, though her cousin seemed younger than that still.

"Then I shall have my fun while I still have the chance," she proclaimed. "Constance, do you have my other lace cuffs?"

Helen located the lace cuffs in a gold gown and carefully removed the stitches holding them there. This was likely not what Mama had in mind when she'd insisted they learn useful needlework as well as fine.

"Patey," Temperance called, "you should see if Helen and Cassandra can do something with that hair of yours."

"I'll bet they can do it in the latest London fashion." Constance's tone, like Temperance's, carried more than a note of teasing.

"I'm happy with my hair the way it is."

Truth be told, her hair was unfortunately low. What would Lord David Beaufort think for the Hayeses to have two maids more fashionable than their own daughter? From the neck up, that was.

Mercy and Verity were more than happy to be fussed over. Helen even styled Verity's hair in a very becoming frizzed pouf. One would think the girl had never had her hair powdered before, she was so giddy.

Patey finally abandoned her chair and strolled over to appraise her sisters. "Will you be using Lord Beaufort to make Winthrop Morley jealous, or simply for fun?" she asked Temperance.

Temper flashed behind Temperance's eyes. "We shall see."

"Perhaps she'll simply lead him along until I'm old enough

to marry," Constance said lightly.

"As if you could keep an interest in a single thing that long, let alone one man."

Patience's words were clearly aimed to cut, but Constance only laughed, a double-syllable, double-step song of condescension. She turned to Temperance. "I'll help you tack in the lace," she said, and they flounced out, arm in arm.

Patience shook her head, watching them go. "I'm afraid they're always like that."

"You don't have to provoke them," Cassandra suggested.

Patience sighed. "It is my fatal flaw."

"We'd be happy to help you get ready," Helen offered.

Patience scanned the room. Verity and Mercy sat on the far bed, furiously discussing something. "I don't know," Patience said at last.

"Please?" Cassandra hoped her smile was encouraging. "We don't have to make you look like your sisters."

Patience glanced back in the direction they'd left, then slowly turned back to Helen and Cassandra. "Yes, but ... could you?"

Helen was more gifted with hair, so she tackled the pomatum and powder while Cassandra pondered the apparel. They had half a dozen gowns to choose from, but these were things they saw every day.

Perhaps Patience needed something new. Cassandra visually measured her cousin's figure. Her gowns might be a little broad across the shoulders for her cousin, but a neckerchief would cover any problems with fit. Cassandra went to her trunk and found her favorite gown, a cream sack-back with stripes, vines and purple grapes, one of the few she hadn't been able to bear to dye. It was a bit overly formal for dinner, but why not? "Here," she said. "Would you like to wear this?"

Patience's countenance lit up, though she couldn't move

while Helen was still pinning her hair up into voluminous curls, now fashionably frizzed. "Such a fine *robe à la française?* Are you sure you don't want to wear that?"

"Oh, yes." Cassandra waved away the idea. How hard did her cousins want to make this transition?

"Thank you," Patience breathed.

Cassandra unpinned Patience's jacket from her stays and helped her out of the sleeves, trading places with Helen to accomplish their jobs. She fetched Helen's purple stomacher and pinned both of their garments to Patience's stays, careful to arrange the extra fabric to not show. It was a bit broad across the back, especially with the weight of the pleated panel that hung down from the shoulders like a train, but as Patience tucked in one of Cassandra's filmiest kerchiefs, the fabric covered any gaping.

Patience stood and slowly spun for them. She was utterly transformed, possibly more beautiful than her sisters, each of whom were lovely. If only she could rid her face of the scowl.

Helen and Cassandra grinned at her, and Patience beamed back.

"Perhaps you'll be the one to steal Lord David's heart," Cassandra suggested.

Patience scoffed. "Not unless he proves to be markedly more intelligent than the other men in this city. But . . . perhaps."

And perhaps serving their cousins wouldn't be so bad after all.

As long as they didn't have to serve the full seven years of an indenture.

Chapter 4

Lord David peered through the darkness into the next tavern. This was the fourth establishment he'd tried today, and it was actually well kept. He was beginning to believe either the coach he'd hired for the day was taking him to the lowest of the low, or the entire city was a hovel behind its brick façades.

He ventured in. The denizens were engaged in active conversation, debating livelily at several tables. While they were obviously not of the *ton*, the patrons were at least clean and decent looking.

Yes, this was promising. He'd already made it further into this tavern than the last three. He approached the counter. "Have you a room?" he asked the keeper.

The tavern keeper gave him a hard stare. "Where are you coming from?"

"Dorset."

The keeper snorted. "Be on your way, then."

"I beg your pardon?"

"We don't serve Tories here."

Lord David's mind scrambled to remember his family's party alignment. He wasn't even certain they *were* Tories; they tried to stay above politics. His strongest opinion of King George was that he dressed plainer than expected. "I—I don't understand."

The tavern keeper leaned on one elbow on the counter, punctuating each word with a poke at the wood. "We don't serve Tories."

He'd had no idea political parties would be so important to the colonists. "My apologies," he managed, though he still wasn't certain what he was apologizing for.

Lord David turned to leave but paused at the threshold. Next to the door, a colored engraving was tacked. It depicted soldiers firing into a crowd of people in a narrow street, blood flowing.

He turned to the nearest patron. "What's this?" he asked.

The man in black homespun snickered until he saw that David genuinely did not know. "The Boston Massacre," he said. "Back in March."

Lord David stared at the picture a long moment. A massacre? In Boston? March—that would have been just when he was leaving England.

The soldiers wore red. There was no mistaking their allegiance.

"Off with you!" the keeper called.

Lord David walked through the door.

These colonies were another world, it seemed. One where soldiers could fire on people in the streets.

He did not know what to make of that in the slightest, beyond feeling unsettled. British soldiers firing on their own citizens?

Could that be why they didn't like Tories? He still wasn't certain what political parties had to do with it. He might not have cared about politics, but what loyal Briton could justify what looked like murder?

He climbed in his coach, but the image and the sense of horror stayed with him.

The next tavern was not promising at first blush. Lord David peered inside, his eyesight adjusting to the dim interior. The air held a whiff of food cooking, but after a moment, the smell sharpened into the scent of something burning, mingled with an odor somewhere between human filth and death.

Where was the proprietor? Perhaps they had one decent room with its own entrance or something to eat that hadn't been charred several inches past the end of its life. It had been hours since his breakfast at the coffeehouse by the docks.

Lord David took shallow breaths and held a handkerchief to his mouth to try to mask the scent. He stepped inside, trying not to disturb any of the patrons.

"'Ey," a gruff voice cried from behind him when he hadn't made it two feet. "Watch yerself."

He turned around to find not a man, as he was expecting, but a woman. Her face and neck seemed to be riddled with pustules. Lord David fell back a step, unable to hide his revulsion.

Was that . . . a pox? "I beg your pardon," he rushed to say, wheeling immediately for the door.

Lord David eased himself back into the coach he'd hired for the day. This was quickly becoming ridiculous. Each tavern was worse than the last. He had no idea what kind of pox that woman had, but he had not come to America to come down with the smallpox.

That place was definitely miasmatic.

He didn't mean to be a fop, but did everywhere in these colonies have to stink of sickness, filth and death? How on earth was he to find a purpose here if he couldn't even find a safe place to stay?

Lord David groaned. Why had he come here? He was tired, hungry, lonely, offended and inconvenienced. Was there no place in this city he could deign to sleep, let alone eat?

He sighed and rested his head against the back wall of the coach. America had not even a single person he could hold a conversation with.

Aside from that Josiah Hayes, the sisters' uncle. Lord David wouldn't qualify it as a conversation, but he had seemed most sincere as he invited him to dinner a second time. Lord David had not really intended to take him up on it, but Hayes was remarkably grateful for the small help he had been.

In England, he never could have admitted to such an acquaintance. But as the morning had proven, he was not in England.

Lord David sat up straight. Enough self-pity. He certainly hadn't come here to wallow. Perhaps it was time to begin thinking like a Pennsylvanian. Or at least thinking where he could eat in relative comfort. He couldn't be certain that would be the Hayes household, but until he could meet someone of a better sort, he had few options.

It had to be nearly two, the time Hayes had said. Lord David leaned out the door to address the driver, directing him to the address Hayes had given: Pine Street in Society Hill.

The trip to the house did not take long, and he knew he had the right place right away. The modest coach that had borne Hayes and his nieces away this morning stood in front of a tidy pink brick house. Hayes himself was climbing from the cab.

His host spotted him quickly. "Oh, good. I was afraid you'd arrive before me," Hayes said.

Apparently, he was expected. Lord David hoped that was a good thing.

Hayes showed him into the drawing room of the house and introduced his neatly dressed wife, who made an elegant enough curtsy for someone of her age. Lord David rewarded her with a bow.

This was already a vast improvement over his morning. He was more than ready to escort her to the dining room when a rustling sounded on the stairs. Lord David looked up to find a brunette beauty in a pink gown and lace cuffs descending. Something about her smile said she knew she looked charming.

Lord David waited for her to arrive before turning to her father, presumably, for introductions, but then another rustling sounded. He patiently waited as another daughter made her entrance, a blonde in a blue gown, then another brunette, much younger, and finally a young girl in blonde ringlets.

Lord David checked with Hayes again, but his host was still watching the stairs. Next came a daughter who had to be somewhere in the middle of the others, quite young, but intensely striking, between her fashionable hairstyle, the lace on her cap, and the fine fabric of her sack-back gown, embellished with purple grapes and vines.

After a pause long enough that he was fairly certain there were no more daughters—what had happened to the nieces?—Lord David consulted Hayes for introductions.

Hayes made no move to present his daughters. Or, rather, he had no time to do so before the eldest, the first to enter, stepped forward and offered her hand. "Temperance Hayes."

She was introducing herself? To him? Lord David looked to Hayes again.

"Apologies, my lord," he said. "We don't have many interactions in the way of nobility here. Introducing one's self is the Pennsylvania way." As if he decided to accommodate his guest, however, Hayes named each of his daughters in turn:

Temperance, Patience (who had lived up to her name by being the last to enter), Constance, Verity and Mercy.

What quaint little names. He had known many Constances and Temperances, but taken together as a set, the effect was charmingly colonial. Lord David greeted each of them, then offered his arm to Mrs. Hayes. Instead, Temperance looped her arm through his.

Either his face did not display the appropriate level of horror, or Temperance had no idea the *faux pas* she had made.

Evidently it was the latter, as her sister Constance took his other elbow, which he hadn't offered to anyone.

"One moment," Hayes said. "My nieces must join us."

Ah, so he would finally be introduced. Lord David attempted to extricate himself from the ladies but couldn't without making one or the other of them feel foolish. So he simply had to steer them around to look to the stairs.

While it was far from the same as seeing someone from Somerset society, after the long, arduous day, he longed to see familiar faces, even if he had not officially made their acquaintances. But he did not recognize the two women who descended the stairs arm in arm. While they'd worn muted colors onboard the *Rimington*, neither of them had ever dressed so plain. Each wore a simple white neckerchief and dark jacket and petticoat, as if they were staff.

From the shoulders up, however, they still wore their hair coiffed and adorned with caps of ribbons and lace.

Was this a joke? He suppressed the urge to laugh.

The sisters instantly recognized him, and whatever horror had been missing from his expression a moment before had found its way to theirs.

"You?" the younger sister said, practically an accusation.

He didn't know the proper response for that greeting, so he settled for "How do you do?"

Lord David could not imagine any way that anyone in the room could be ignorant of the sheer rage radiating off the sisters, clearly aimed at him. He was, however, ignorant as to why.

Unless it was because he'd allowed them to be marched off to be sold this morning. That might have something to do with it. But hadn't he helped them in the end by sending their uncle to their rescue?

He checked with Hayes, who was occupied with staring in wonderment at his own nieces. At least Lord David was not the only one perplexed by their attire.

"Uh, Lord David, allow me to present my nieces, Helen and Cassandra Crofton. Ladies, allow me to present Lord David Beaufort."

He disentangled himself from the Hayes daughters to bow to the Croftons. Helen, the elder, returned the courtesy; the younger sister did not.

"Ah, and now we have a name for Your Worshipfulness," said Cassandra. Yes, she'd always delighted in taunting him. He actually found himself not disliking it this time.

Cassandra dropped into a low curtsy worthy of King George's court. Whatever she was wearing, the lady did have proper bearing.

Temperance threaded her arm through his again. "Shall we, Your . . . Worship?"

Oh, what had Cassandra done to these poor colonials? "'Lord David' will suffice."

She beamed at him. Before her sister could seize his other elbow, he maneuvered to his hostess and offered in no uncertain terms.

Anne Hayes accepted with a gracious smile. Hayes escorted his nieces, and they made their way into the dining hall. The cream-colored paneled walls were quite fashionable, actually, as were the wallpaper accents with scrolling designs and paintings.

Perhaps he could admit to knowing these people.

As soon as he seated her mother, Constance maneuvered to the chair next to him at the table. He glanced again at the Croftons' laughable *ensembles*. On second thought, perhaps he ought to reserve judgment for the moment.

Cassandra Isabelle Artemis Crofton had never been so humiliated in all her life, her cousins' breaches of etiquette notwithstanding.

How could Uncle Josiah have invited this popinjay here to see their low estate? Only a few hours before, they had been a gentleman's daughters, and then they were ladies' maids for a provincial lawyer, and now *Lord David* had to be here to witness it.

She couldn't miss the mirth that danced in his eyes each time he looked their way throughout the first course. She stabbed her orange fool with her spoon far more viciously than the dessert warranted. He would never treat her with the respect she deserved.

She hadn't decided whether this Pennsylvanian custom of having the staff sit at the table with the family made things better or worse, but even Polly was seated with them.

Did Cassandra have to be seated directly across from their guest?

"Lord David," Temperance began, her voice coy and treacly, "is Beaufort your title?"

"No, Beaufort is my surname."

"Oh, then what is your title?"

Cassandra tried not to watch him but couldn't tear her gaze away as his smile grew brittle. "Ah, that would be my father with a title. The Marquess of Dorset."

A marquess? They'd been humbled before the son of a marquess? Cassandra jabbed her spoon into her fool so hard it clanked against the bottom of the porcelain bowl, attracting Lord David's attention. She forced herself to smile back.

A marquess! Why, they'd once entertained a royal duke for two weeks at Heartcomb!

"Wouldn't that make you an earl?" Constance asked from his other side.

Lord David offered a polite chuckle. "That would be my eldest brother, George." When Constance still looked at him expectantly, he added, "The Earl of Somerset."

Constance beamed. Cassandra's first impulse was to rail against this new injustice—he was not even the heir to the marquess?—until she saw something else in his eyes.

Was that . . . hurt? The popinjay felt pain?

Well, of course he did. She'd never imagined he hadn't. She simply hadn't cared.

"Your Magnificence," she said, addressing him, "is Dorset nice this time of year?"

"Yes, it's lovely." His voice was wistful, and for a moment, Cassandra thought of her own home at Heartcomb. Spring was the most beautiful time there, when all the trees came into flower.

When her mind returned to the room, she realized Lord David was still looking at her. "Cassandra," he finally finished.

Of all the impertinence. He had only just bothered to learn her name, and she had never given him leave to use her given name. "Your Preeminence." She added as much sugar to her tone as she could. "We are not on intimate terms."

"My apologies." He added sarcasm to an already condescending tone. "Cassie."

"Well," Aunt Anne said, "I believe it is time for us to retire."

Cassandra checked the plates around the table. She was the only one who hadn't finished, and her dining experience was truly a waste of something as rare as an orange. Polly hopped up to begin clearing.

Cassandra stood also. "I'll help."

"Oh, that's not necessary, thank you." Polly took the bowl from Cassandra. Cassandra checked with Aunt Anne, who motioned for her to come with them.

They weren't to clear the dishes, then? Cassandra and Helen obeyed, trailing behind their cousins dutifully.

Aunt Anne led them all upstairs and simply gestured at the bedroom. They had left it in disarray, hair powder and pomatum tins out on the open wardrobes, three gowns strewn across the beds.

"Sorry, Aunt Anne," Helen said. They both hurried to begin straightening up.

"No need to apologize," Aunt Anne said. "The girls leave it this way every day." She gestured at the room again, and her daughters flitted around, setting it to rights instantly.

"That isn't necessary," Helen said. "We could do it."

"We are truly grateful for your help," Aunt Anne said, speaking as if she were picking her words carefully. "But you certainly aren't any more responsible than they are."

Cassandra wasn't quite sure that was accurate; they had left the things out.

Aunt Anne again seemed to be choosing her words carefully, or perhaps she always spoke with such intention and care. "Why did you choose these gowns, my nieces?"

Helen and Cassandra exchanged a glance. "For work, naturally," Helen said.

"Did you think that dinner with Lord David would require

work?"

"Well, um." Helen silently conferred with Cassandra.

"We aren't certain what our duties are to be," Cassandra said.

"Duties?" Aunt Anne's eyebrows drew together.

"In the household?" Cassandra tried.

Aunt Anne was no less confused.

"As staff," Helen finished.

Aunt Anne startled, her mobcap bobbing slightly. "Why would you be staff?"

Cassandra's gaze fell, and she assumed Helen was looking down as well. "Uncle Josiah had to buy our indenture this morning."

"What?" Aunt Anne turned to the stairs, as if Uncle Josiah would appear to affirm everything they said. But then she shook her head. "I assure you, nieces, we do not believe in bound labor."

Cassandra's head flew up so fast she nearly lost her cap. "Beg pardon?"

"Whatever Josiah might have paid, we have no intention of owning an indenture."

Helen and Cassandra looked at one another. They were free?

And they'd dressed like this in front of Lord David Beaufort for nothing?

Helen and Cassandra had no other alternative but to burst into laughter. At least they would never see His Pompousness Lord Popinjay again.

"Oh, gracious," Temperance said. "We were afraid you were some sort of Puritans!"

"Or worse," Patience added, "New Englanders."

"Let's get you out of those things," Constance agreed.

As their cousins flocked around them, the truth set in: they were really free. They hadn't fallen in station at all. Cassandra met Helen's eyes, and the message passed unspoken between them. Yes, this could be their home.

Chapter 5

*L*ord David stood when the ladies left. He was surprisingly sorry to see Cassandra go, just when he was beginning to enjoy sparring with her.

Hayes reseated himself at the table and gestured for Lord David to join him. "I don't mean to keep you from your business," Lord David said.

"Quite all right, my lord. I'm happy to entertain as long as you'd wish to stay. But I don't intend to keep *you* from your own work."

"I do need to be about finding a place to lodge."

"Are you hoping for something temporary, or more permanent?"

That was the question, wasn't it? "I'm not entirely certain," he admitted.

Hayes studied him a moment. Perhaps he shouldn't have owned that. "I have a flat to let above my law office. It's in the center of town, near the State House."

"Oh." He had not expected to receive an offer, but perhaps Providence was smiling upon him. "I appreciate that very much. Shall we talk terms?"

Hayes nodded with what seemed to be his usual equanimity. "Certainly, but first, may I ask what brought you to the colonies?"

"The very question I keep posing myself," he murmured.

"What was that?"

"Nothing, apologies. I'm still trying to determine what exactly I shall do here."

"I see," Hayes said. "And what do you mean to do?"

Lord David straightened. This man went right to the heart of the matter, didn't he? He watched Hayes for a moment longer. He didn't know much about this man, but he had already been amply generous. "I mean to make something of myself."

A slow grin suffused Hayes's features. "That's precisely why I came to the colonies. I thought such things came in battle." His smile stilled and faded. "I'm glad you're not laboring under the same misapprehension."

Lord David gave him a small nod of thanks. He wasn't sure he deserved the praise; had there been a war on, he might very well have attempted that route.

The image of the engraving from this morning emerged in his mind, the red blood and the red coats. War was not a good fit for him.

"Now, why does the son of a marquess need to make something of himself?"

Lord David allowed a little laugh, although he knew the question was sincere. "The third son."

"Ah."

Yes, they had the heir, the spare and the err, as he'd unfortunately heard his father quip regularly. Far from the only time he'd known his father's scorn.

"So, business?" Hayes asked. "Law? Politics?"

"Not politics," he said quickly. That had never been his strong suit, and he'd already had his fill of colonial politics—and seen how poorly he'd fared. "I'm afraid I'm not suited to the law either. Perhaps business."

"Excellent," Hayes said. "I have a few friends I could introduce you to, once you decide."

"Thank you very much. This is really very kind of you."

"Not at all. It's simply that you . . . remind me of someone."

Could he have known his father? People often said he favored him as a child, though Lord David failed to see the resemblance. "Where in England are you from?"

"Surrey."

Probably not then. "Lovely county."

"Yes, it was." Hayes coughed in the way of a man covering emotion. "Look at that, you've made me go all sentimental." He shook his head. "I'd offer you sherry, but my wife was raised a Quaker."

"Understood," Lord David said, though he didn't understand the first thing about Quakers. As soon as he felt the slightest bit at ease in Philadelphia, he had to be reminded that he, too, was very far from home.

He cleared his throat. "What type of business do your friends deal in?"

Within half an hour, Helen and Cassandra were dressed in their own clothes again. Aunt Anne had retired to her room, leaving them to talk with their cousins, and they were finally at ease with them, though Cassandra still strove to put the right name with the right girl.

"How do you know Lord David?" Temperance asked.

"We were on the same ship for the crossing." Helen's answer was clipped. Clearly her opinion of Lord David was no better than Cassandra's.

Constance—she was easy to remember—threw herself back onto the bed as if fainting. "Isn't he handsome?"

Cassandra gave a begrudging nod.

"Do you think he'll write to me?"

"Certainly not," Helen said. "He must be ten years your senior, and we shall never see him again."

"Come," Verity said, "Let us show you the garden. It is the biggest in the whole city."

Her older sisters all exchanged a glance that indicated that was hyperbole. But Cassandra realized she could suddenly breathe again. It had been months since she'd seen any quantity of greenery. The shrubbery in front of the Hayeses' home was nothing compared to the estate at Heartcomb. Hopefully the back garden had a little space.

Helen was equally enthused. "Yes, please."

Their cousins let Cassandra and Helen lead the way down the stairs. Cassandra reached the landing behind the door first—and ran directly into Lord David Beaufort, clearly on his way out.

This was a habit she had better break quickly, or it would likely break her. How did the man have such sharp elbows?

"I beg your pardon!" He straightened his coat.

"Oh, no, Your Mercifulness." Cassandra offered her deepest curtsy yet. "It is I who must beg *your* forgiveness."

When she straightened again, she saw the ire and the ice in his clear blue eyes—and for once, she felt no satisfaction.

"If you are a gentleman's daughter," he said in a low voice, "you ought to know how to treat your betters. Clearly your cousins know how to show better respect than you do."

From the corner of her eye, she caught the curtsies her

cousins offered: perfectly acceptable for polite company. Finally, she understood why he was censuring her so. She had embarrassed Lord David. And he had done nothing to deserve it.

At least not since this morning. Or dinner.

Before she could muster an appropriate apology, however, the door flew open. Lord David was chivalrous enough to pull her out of the way with one hand—if a little roughly—and catch the swinging door with the other, closing it behind a diminutive maid.

"Ginny?" Uncle Josiah addressed the newcomer.

"Sorry, sir, I know I should have been here."

"Are you quite well?" he asked.

She was awfully thin, but Cassandra suspected that might always be the case, as her jacket wasn't falling off her shoulders.

"I am, sir," Ginny said, "but my cousins." She gulped. "It's the smallpox."

A collective gasp sounded. The smallpox? Here?

"Where do they live?" Uncle Josiah was more insistent than Cassandra had ever seen him. Though, to be fair, she had only met him this morning.

"Germantown."

Aunt Anne turned to Cassandra and Helen. "Have you ladies had the smallpox?"

"We have." Cassandra offered her forearm where the most prominent scars were.

"A relief, to be sure," Uncle Josiah said.

"We'll send the little girls to my sister's," Aunt Anne said, her gentle voice sure. "That should be far enough away."

"You know how a miasma spreads." Uncle Josiah and Aunt Anne consulted one another and seemed to come to a silent agreement. "We shall have to inoculate them."

"You inoculate in the colonies?" Lord David spoke for the first time since Ginny's arrival. He suddenly did not seem quite well either.

"Of course." Amusement filled Uncle Josiah's voice. "Did you think science hadn't crossed the Atlantic?"

"Oh, no," Lord David rushed to reassure him. The surprise still on his countenance, however, clearly told a different story.

"You've had the smallpox?" Aunt Anne asked Lord David. The dear woman was willing to ask after this perfect stranger?

"I?" Lord David gave a little, uncomfortable laugh. "I've not."

Cassandra and Helen startled in unison. Even Uncle Josiah seemed to be gaping at him. "A man—a nobleman—of England who has never had the smallpox?" Uncle Josiah wondered. "Now there is a rare breed."

"From a family excessively cautious of miasmas." His smile was tight.

"Well, how fortunate for you." Aunt Anne's gentle tone was encouraging.

"Yes, until now, it seems." Lord David scanned the room again, his gaze finally landing on first Cassandra, then Ginny, who scuttled away toward the kitchen. "Thank you again for dinner. Good day." He bowed quickly from the neck.

Cassandra and her family returned the courtesy, and Lord David departed.

Temperance and Constance bustled over to the tall windows to watch his retreat. Cassandra shared a wry look with her sister. If their cousins knew Lord David as they did, they would be more eager to see him go than to watch him leave.

Of course, Cassandra had only just learned his name this afternoon.

He must have set off quickly because they didn't watch for

long before bounding back over to Cassandra. "I can't believe you know him. Did you see his wig?" Temperance pointed out. "White as snow."

Constance took her sister's arm. "I wonder what color his hair is."

"It's dark," Cassandra supplied. Why? She should have ignored their silly nattering or changed the subject.

Constance's and Temperance's attention snapped to her. "When did you see his hair?"

"When he lost another wig over the side of the boat, along with his dinner."

"He dropped his plate *and* his wig off the ship? How sad." Mercy frowned.

Cassandra and Helen silently conferred but decided to spare their youngest cousin the less pleasant meaning.

"Oh, how romantic." Constance sighed, clasping both hands to her heart. "To fall in love at sea!"

"Sea travel was not romantic." Cassandra tried to make her tone apologetic, but there was nothing "romantic" about spending weeks trapped in a tiny, stifling room, avoiding a certain rude nobleman, subsisting on sailors' rations. She still felt queasy on dry land.

"Nor was Lord David," Helen assured them. "He was quite ... severe to us."

"Oh." Temperance's countenance darkened as if she immediately changed her mind about him.

"Should I not have invited him?" Uncle Josiah asked. The concern on his kind face mirrored a look Cassandra had seen on her mother so many times, and her heart caught in her chest.

She would never see her mother's grave again.

"It is your home, Uncle," Helen answered for her. "We're merely guests."

"Guests? Why, no. You're part of our family. I only wanted to thank him for helping me to find you this morning."

What? Cassandra looked to Helen, who was equally shocked, and back to Uncle Josiah. "He helped you?"

"Yes, he showed me where they had taken you. The scoundrels." His normally serene features tightened into a scowl.

This made no sense. The man who had been nothing but a snob, snubbing them for the last nine weeks, then refused to do the chivalrous, proper thing in rescuing them from being sold... was the same man who had helped to save them? When he had no reason to whatsoever?

"I've a good mind to bring up a suit. How many other innocents have they dragged to that slave market unawares?"

"Do you think Cousin Lowell paid our whole fare then?" Helen asked.

Uncle Josiah pondered it a long moment. "I don't know Lowell, so I cannot say. It was still criminal."

"All slavery is immoral," Aunt Anne said. She condemned the practice with such equanimity she might have been offering tea rather than a controversial opinion.

"Of course, dear." Uncle Josiah took her hand. "I have an item of business I must attend to. I'll be home before supper."

The girls ran to give their father a kiss and filed out. Cassandra wasn't quite sure how to take leave of their new guardian, and Helen gave her an expression that felt equally lost.

"Goodbye, my dears." Uncle Josiah nodded to them, squeezed Aunt Anne's hand, and departed.

"Does he always work this much?"

"Josiah has become a sought-after lawyer in business affairs. His expertise is much valued throughout the New World." Aunt Anne beckoned for them to follow, offering her

54

elbows. "Come, see the garden."

Cassandra and Helen accepted, and as they walked back through the house, Cassandra did not think about the fact that Lord David had helped them for some reason this morning. At least not very much.

Chapter 6

*W*hat were they doing here? Her first night in the colonies, and Cassandra could not sleep. Every time she lay still, she felt as if she were back on the ship in those first days, rolling on the waves.

She might be ill, and not just with homesickness.

She rolled over to Helen, peacefully asleep in the moonlight. How very unfair. She had spent the same amount of time on a boat. Why should she be spared the same torment?

Was Lord David lying awake wherever he was, or was Cassandra the only one to suffer so?

Cassandra groaned and rolled back over. Her undulating stomach convinced her that this position wouldn't help either.

It wasn't merely the physical misery, either. She couldn't help the feeling that she had made a terrible mistake today. In offending Lord David? In coming to the colonies? In leaving her home? She hadn't had a choice in most of those, but that didn't mean she'd done right.

She had spent so long focused on surviving the crossing that she had never considered what their life should become once they arrived. What on earth was she to do with herself? At Heartcomb, she had had a purpose, a function. She was supposed to help care for the tenants and the community. She'd spent time in charity for the poor, in tending the sick, in helping around their home.

When she awoke tomorrow, she could not be much assistance with any of those things. With seven other women about—not including the staff—there were surely already hands for every task that might need doing.

Did she have a place in this entire continent?

She certainly had no place on any other. Cousin Lowell had made that clear. Did she have a choice?

What became of a gentleman's daughter when she was orphaned?

She pulled herself from the bed and fetched her wrapper off her trunk to put over her chemise. Her first night in an unfamiliar house, she didn't quite know where she was going or how to get there in the dark. She simply knew she couldn't stay here.

Did "here" mean this bed or this continent?

The dark stairs were treacherous, but a faint light glowed at the bottom. She crept along slowly, leaning against the wall, until she reached the landing.

The landing where she'd run into Lord David this afternoon.

She tried not to remember that embarrassing moment too long.

The warm glow proved to be coming from a low fire in the grate. Someone sat in a chair before the fire, but Cassandra couldn't tell whom from the silhouette.

"Who's there?" she called softly.

The person whirled around. Uncle Josiah. "Oh, child. Are you quite well?"

"Yes, Uncle. I can't sleep, though." She pressed a hand to her stomach. "I feel as though I'm—"

"Still on the boat," Uncle Josiah finished for her. In the embers' light, she could barely make out a soft kind of nostalgia in Uncle Josiah's smile. "I understand." He gestured for her to take a seat opposite him. "Come. Sit."

Cassandra settled in the other wingback armchair facing the massive marble fireplace and let the fire's warmth radiate into her. The nights were still cool in May in Philadelphia.

She addressed Uncle Josiah. "You can't sleep either?"

He sighed, staring into the embers. "No. The smallpox. We'll have to have the girls inoculated quickly, of course, it's only that—Anne is . . . I don't know if she can nurse them this time."

Cassandra tried to infer his meaning. Surely Aunt Anne couldn't be with child at her age. "Is she unwell?"

"She tires so quickly now," Uncle Josiah explained. "Tonight she was asleep practically before she lay down. I can't imagine how she could stand being on her feet all day." He offered a little chortle at his own pun.

"What will you do?"

"Think on it further." He leaned forward and retrieved the poker to stir the coals.

Perhaps that was why Aunt Anne was always so gentle—she hadn't the strength to do more.

And Uncle Josiah had still agreed to take in two more mouths to feed? "Thank you for taking us in," Cassandra murmured. "I know it's a hardship, too."

"My sister's girls? To be sure. Not a moment's hesitation, for me or Anne."

"Thank you." She pulled her wrapper closer, and finally dared ask the question that had worn away at her mind since that afternoon. "Did Lord David really tell you where to find us?"

"Yes. Why?"

"He simply did not seem overly disposed toward us on the journey."

"So you said. Well, he seems like someone who has a few things he's still coming to understand."

Cassandra looked to the fire. That was certainly a generous way of thinking of him. "I don't suppose we'll see him again." Why did that thought not make her heart light?

"On the contrary. He's let the flat above my office, so I'll be seeing him, anyway."

Cassandra vowed that if she ever knew she'd have to see Lord David again, she would make up for her ridiculous showing today.

Once again, that prospect wasn't as unwelcome as she'd expected.

"It must be very difficult to feel... superfluous, even in one's own family," Uncle Josiah continued. Cassandra looked up at him, worried he might mean her, but he added, "For Lord David."

"Yes." Was that how he felt? She recalled the brittle smile, the pain as he'd mentioned his family. And then she'd gone and insulted him. Perhaps he had been right. That was hardly conduct becoming a gentleman's daughter.

"You know, I was his age when I came here," Uncle Josiah mused. "And even more naïve, believe it or not."

Lord David, naïve? That was one epithet she hadn't applied to him.

Uncle Josiah continued. "He seem to have a quick enough mind. If he is able to apply himself and put his time to good use, I'm sure he'll find purpose in his life soon."

Cassandra drew a breath. That was precisely what she needed. Purpose. Direction.

Those sorts of things were simple for a man. A woman cared for hearth and home, and if she didn't have that, nor tenants nor charity work to keep her busy, what would she do with her time? Sit by the fire and knit?

She didn't even know how to knit. Mama had always said needlework was more useful.

She drew her knees up to her chest, gathering her wrapper over herself. She wasn't even certain of their position in the community. Certainly there were no estates like Heartcomb. This place was far more like London, all city. How ever would she find people to help here? Let alone friends?

At least she had Helen. And her cousins seemed nice, if a strange mix of flighty and dour.

Did they have a purpose?

Did she?

Uncle Josiah poked the fire again.

"Did he find it?" Cassandra asked.

"Hm?"

"Did Lord David find his purpose?"

Uncle Josiah didn't answer at first. "I think he will, in time. If he learns to adapt to his life here."

Cassandra pondered that for a long moment. Perhaps she had been too quick to judge Lord David. It seemed they had more in common than she'd thought. She had no choice but to adapt to her life here as well.

Would there be a place for her? She didn't have Helen's nature, always forging ahead, sure of herself. She could match wits with a man like Lord David, dance with a man like Lord David, even—heaven forbid—marry a man like Lord David. Those things might give her a household, a position in society, a name. But none of them would *matter*.

Had she ever cared about this before? She'd always known her place at home. She was the younger daughter of Thomas

Crofton, a gentleman. She was a mistress of Heartcomb.

That was her position and her place. They had given her something to occupy her time. None of those was a purpose.

Was that something she could find in the colonies?

She turned to her uncle, who was pondering the fire. "Why did you come to the colonies?"

"Hm?" He perked up as if his deliberating had really been dozing.

She repeated the question.

"Oh. I came for glory." He snorted. "Your Uncle William and I thought we would find it in the war."

She had heard only the vaguest stories of Uncle William. Mostly, she knew he'd died as a soldier. Brave. Honorable. Loyal.

But Uncle Josiah did not sound patriotic right now. He simply sounded sad. "We didn't find it, if you were curious."

"I'm sorry."

Uncle Josiah merely nodded. "I was going home to Surrey when I met Anne. I had never known anyone so gentle. She was the salve I needed."

That sounded much sweeter than her own parents' story, having met at a country dance. She'd always found that romantic, though not quite as rapturously as Constance probably would have. Still, her parents had married for love as well.

"Do you miss it?" Cassandra's voice was barely above a whisper.

"Yes," Uncle Josiah said. "But I have a life here, and I should miss that much more were I ever to leave."

"Not your family?"

"I would never leave without them, my dear. But this is our home."

Cassandra turned back to the embers, which were steadily

growing colder. Would she ever feel that way about this place? She wasn't sure, but she was starting to hope so. What other choice did she have?

"Did you find purpose?" Cassandra asked. "After the war?"

"Oh yes."

"In Aunt Anne?"

A soft smile pulled at one corner of his mouth. "In a way, yes. But also our children, and my work, helping people. It's good to feel needed, as though you're a part of something. A community."

Yes. She might not have been needed, but she had felt as though she was a part of a community at Heartcomb. Of course she didn't have that here after a single day. "Did it take you long to find that community?"

Uncle Josiah's eyebrows raised as though he were surprised by the question. "I suppose it did take a while. Hard to say, child. It's the work of a lifetime."

Cassandra pondered that a moment. Her stomach was finally beginning to settle.

"It's good that you're here now," he said. "With the smallpox in Germantown, Ginny's family may need her help."

"Does she live in Germantown?"

"She lives here." Uncle Josiah eased back in his chair. "Her cousins live in Germantown. Six of them, all very young. Her aunt married a German."

Obviously Germantown had earned its name from its settlers' origin. "And they'll need Ginny?"

"They'll need all the help they can get."

Cassandra pondered that for a long moment. Somewhere help was needed.

How many times had Mama gone to help a poor local family in need of aid when sickness befell them? Cassandra had been too young to accompany her most of the time, but she'd learned a few things from her.

Perhaps that was what she was meant to do. She would have to ponder on this more. She leaned her head against the wing of the armchair.

"I'm sure you're very tired," Uncle Josiah said.

At his words, she jolted awake. Had she dozed off? "Would you like me to sit up with you?"

"No need. I won't be much longer." He reached into his waistcoat and withdrew a flask.

"I thought Aunt Anne said your family abstains from alcohol."

He looked over at her, a spark of mischief in his eyes. "Don't tell her."

Cassandra pressed one finger to her lips.

Yes, she decided as she climbed the stairs. She felt much more settled. She would find a purpose. And, for his sake, she hoped the same for Lord David.

Chapter 7

*L*ord David sat at the large desk he'd been supplied in Josiah Hayes's apartment, poring over the papers he'd collected over the last three weeks. Reports from several of Hayes's friends and associates and clients, not merely sales reports, but business accounts.

Lord David had not been a terrible student for the tutor his family had hired away from Harrow, and mathematics had been a particularly strong subject for him. And yet neither of those things were making this decision easier.

He wasn't sure that directly getting involved in trade was quite fitting, or quite his forte. He knew he wanted to begin investing. But somehow there had to be a way to support these businesses and also make money of his own.

Really, the question was not how but which—which of all these trades was something he might conceivably manage? Or was that not it?

A knock sounded at his door. "Come," he said, without looking up from his papers.

"Good afternoon, Lord David."

That was not the voice he'd been expecting. Rather than his valet, Josiah Hayes stood in the doorway to his study.

"Oh, how do you do?" Lord David rose halfway. "Do sit."

"Thank you." Hayes took the seat in front of his desk. "Very nice bookcases."

Lord David glanced at the only furnishings he'd had time to purchase thus far, flanking the room with most of the books he'd brought with him. A rug and a few more bookcases and the study would be quite serviceable. "Thank you."

"How are your investments coming along?"

"I have some decisions to make." Lord David tried to keep the tenor of the conversation positive. "Can I do anything for you?" Occasionally, his landlord came up from his law office downstairs simply to visit.

Lord David had little enough company that he looked forward to these visits as much as meals.

"I came to see how you were faring."

"Well, several of these businesses seem very strong. It's quite difficult to choose among them."

Hayes picked up a paper. "How about this one?"

Lord David checked the page. Atop the ledger notes was another note: *Flour mill*, he'd written. *Germantown*.

"That one looks a little uncertain for me." He took the page and set it to the side. He wouldn't go risking his life for his investments.

"What criteria are you using to evaluate?"

"Distance from the miasma, for one."

Hayes chuckled. "Yes, we'll surely want to steer you clear of that. Are you considering inoculation?"

"Yes. In fact, Dr. Rush will be here to do it in two days."

"That was quick."

"Indeed." Lord David had sought out the physician as soon as he'd had his trunks unloaded in his apartment, but he'd had no idea how extensive the preparations would be. And Dr. Rush said that other doctors would require him to spend several more weeks preparing his body for the illness.

"Dr. Rush is an excellent choice."

"He came highly recommended." His valet had spent minutes extolling Dr. Rush's credentials, from an M.D. from the University of Edinburgh to serving as a professor at the College of Philadelphia Medical School. It had been the most Westing had ever said to him.

"Do you have anyone to care for you?" Hayes asked.

He regarded the older man for a moment. Josiah Hayes cared how he fared beyond business?

"My valet," Lord David answered. He'd finally found help after an entire week of having to dress himself like some commoner. It had been bad enough on the boat.

Josiah studied him for a long moment. Was that not an acceptable answer? "Good," he finally said. "Inoculations are nothing to be trifled with. You're lucky you came at the right time of year."

That was another thing he hadn't been aware of. The science of inoculation had been perfected to the proper season, proper preparation, proper treatment. And still one in fifty died.

The rest—most of the rest—would become dreadfully ill for weeks, but recover, the sickness purged from their bodies, leaving only a few scars.

The unlucky few would have nothing happen. They would have to endure the process again, or risk the far deadlier full smallpox.

Lord David wasn't sure whether he would rather fall in the former group or the later. The preparations had hardly been enjoyable—odd changes to his diet—but the idea of being bedbound for weeks, fighting off an illness that could still kill him. . . .

"I look forward to it being finished," he said.

"As you should. Will you be making any investments beforehand?"

A part of his mind hounded him, telling him he shouldn't make investments, in the event that the unthinkable did happen. But, honestly, it was of little consequence to him if his investments outlived him. He had no heirs, and his family certainly had no need of the few pounds he was prepared to lend.

For a man as rich as he was, somehow, he had very little to lose.

He cleared his throat. "I hope so." He tossed the papers aside. "These are all good investments that are sure to make plenty of money. I simply cannot decide."

Josiah cocked his head, one eyebrow raised ever so slightly. "Cannot? Or will not?"

Lord David straightened in his seat. Was he questioning— he took a deep breath and fought back the tide of indignation. "What do you mean?"

"Well, these businesses are all sound investments, or I would not have sent them to you. I meant only that perhaps there's something more you're looking for than you'll find in these papers."

Lord David nodded slowly. What on earth else did he intend to use his wealth for if not to increase his purse? Was there some other reason for business in America?

If there were, Josiah would know. "What would you recommend?" Lord David asked.

"I can't say for certain if even you don't know what you're looking for. But I suggest meeting with each of the owners of your topmost choices. That might give you a clearer path forward."

"How does one meet with a business owner to make an investment if one is not actually making the investment yet?"

Josiah laughed. "That is one you'll have to figure out, I'm afraid. But I'm sure you'll find a way."

"Thank you for your confidence."

A knock sounded at the door, and Westing, his valet, stepped in. "Miss Cassandra Crofton is here for Mr. Hayes, my lord."

Cassandra was here? Surely she meant to wait in the drawing room for her uncle to leave, but he wanted to see her. "Show her in." Lord David motioned for her to be admitted, and his rib cage seemed to constrict as he stood. He couldn't imagine why. Unless perhaps it was because he hadn't seen anyone he'd known longer than three weeks in... three weeks.

She hardly counted.

Cassandra stepped in and offered a perfect curtsy before looking to her uncle. Her hair was curled and swept up underneath a violet-trimmed straw hat, and her fashionable sack-back gown had clearly come with her from England, though Lord David felt sure he'd seen it before, and not aboard the *Rimington*.

"Miss Crofton," he greeted her before she could address Josiah. He braced himself for whatever clever remark she might fire off at him.

"Apologies, my lord," she said. She seemed... sincere. "I hope I'm not interrupting anything terribly important."

"No, no," Lord David reassured her. "Merely chatting about business."

"Ah." For perhaps the first time, she regarded him with something like respect. "Have you found your purpose?"

He paused for a moment, tilting his head to the side. Though she certainly meant the reason for their meeting or the intent of his business, he couldn't help but think she intended something deeper with that word.

Or perhaps he simply thought that because he was so desperate to find his own purpose here.

"And what is *your* purpose here, my dear?" Josiah asked, teasing in his tone.

"I was sent to find you, Uncle."

"Then you have succeeded." Rather than anger at interrupting their meeting, informal though it might have been, Josiah's face held only warmth for his niece.

How must that have felt?

"We were hoping you might come," she said. The last word seemed to hold some additional meaning which Josiah quickly caught.

"Oh, yes, that's today. Certainly." He bowed to Lord David. "Good luck, my lord."

"Thank you for coming," Lord David said.

Josiah nodded, but Cassandra didn't acknowledge him.

"Both of you," he added. Her eyebrows crinkled together almost imperceptibly before she dropped into another curtsy and left with her uncle.

What? No repartee? Well, their prior conversations were mostly alternating insults, but he found himself missing her wit all the same. Were they not friends?

No, he supposed they were not.

He moved to the window to watch them leave the building from the story below him. Before she boarded the coach, Cassandra lifted her gaze and saw him. She quickly looked away and allowed her uncle to hand her into the coach.

That had been foolish of him. Why had he wanted to see her again? Yes, he'd known her a few months, but she was no real connection to home.

Moreover, she was frustrating and pretentious. He did not

even like her, he reminded himself.

Or did he? If she now regarded him with respect, something had changed.

Lord David finally returned to his desk after Cassandra's coach disappeared down the street, the distraction gone at last. He should probably endeavor to avoid her.

Unless perhaps she no longer hated him? She cared to ask about his purpose, and the look in her eyes today suggested she could feel something other than loathing for him.

He would have to find out. Some sort of gesture or gift, perhaps, to attract her attention. Silk for a new gown? Westing could tell him if such a thing was done in the colonies. She could probably use it to replace her dyed wardrobe if she was out of mourning now. The gown and petticoat she'd worn today had grapes and vines on cream fabric.

She looked very well in it. She should have more like it. Yes. Silk for a gown and petticoat. As soon as this inoculation business was over.

He turned back to his work, reading over the papers again and casting each summary aside. Any of these businesses could double his investment.

A large purse did not a purpose make.

"No," he murmured to himself, finally answering Cassandra's question. "I've not found my purpose."

Chapter 8

Two days after he saw Cassandra, Lord David admitted a different kind of visitor to his study: Dr. Benjamin Rush. Though Dr. Rush couldn't be any older than Lord David, he knew the doctor was the right choice, well educated, well respected. Rumor had it Benjamin Franklin had personally selected the doctor to fund his education in Britain.

And yet his stomach seemed to veritably crawl.

"Good day," Dr. Rush greeted him. "Are we ready?"

Lord David drew a deep breath and managed a curt nod.

This was not the same thing as having the smallpox. This was much safer, and it would rid his system of the disease. He would not die.

Unlike Georgette.

Those were merely his mother's fears talking, and it was a small wonder, as he'd had little else from her. He hadn't even known his sister Georgette; she'd died before he was born.

He shook off the thoughts and turned to Dr. Rush. "Shall we?" He gestured toward the door. Surely this was something done in a bedroom, not one serving as a study.

"Oh, we can do the procedure here. It will take only a moment." He gestured to the chair. "Please, sit."

Lord David obeyed. "Shall I take off my coat?"

"Shouldn't be necessary."

Was this process not as extensive as he'd been led to believe? He'd heard other doctors slit one's arms and placed a thread with the ... diseased material on it inside the wound for days.

Dr. Rush set his case on an empty spot on the desk. As if the doctor had read his mind, he said, "This is the latest method practiced in London. It's just as effective as the thread method, but less prone to other infection." He leaned a bit closer to add, "And it hurts less."

The momentary pain of the procedure was not Lord David's primary concern, but he appreciated the information all the same. "So I'll still be ill?"

"Yes, but there are often fewer pustules with this method."

Another small victory, he supposed. "How is it done, this new method?"

"Your hand, please?"

Lord David gave it. Dr. Rush removed a lancet from his case, double-checking the sharp ends. With a quick jab, he inserted the blade just under the skin on the back of the hand at the base of Lord David's thumb. He removed the lancet and gestured for the other hand.

"That's all?"

Dr. Rush repeated the procedure with the other end of the lancet. "That's all."

"Hm." That had only stung.

"The hard part is what comes next. Try to avoid any places of infection—in fact, best to stay in. It could take up to two weeks for the illness to begin its course."

"And if it fails?"

Dr. Rush dropped the lancet in his case and snapped it shut. "Then we try again."

"Thank you." He held out his hand to shake but hesitated. "No bandages?"

"No, best to leave them open."

Interesting.

"I shall be back to check on your progress regularly," Dr. Rush promised on his way out, "but should you need anything in the meantime, your valet knows where to call."

"Yes, thank you." Lord David stood as he left and settled again at his desk.

As soon as Westing returned from showing Dr. Rush out, he looked at Lord David with solicitous concern. "Do you mean to lie down, sir?" he asked.

"I mean to finish my work." He picked up a quill pen but found holding it was awkward with the fresh slice in his skin. At least it wasn't making a mess.

"Could I be your scribe, sir?" Westing offered.

"That would be excellent, thank you."

He had never had to give much thought to how much he paid his staff—his father's domain—but he vowed to make sure he was paying Westing above the going rate.

"You're certain you don't wish to convalesce?" Westing asked.

"Thank you, no. I'm certain I shall have plenty of time for that soon enough."

Westing nodded.

"You've had the smallpox, haven't you?"

"The inoculation, yes, sir." He tapped his upper arm in the same spot Lord David had expected to receive the cuts.

"Good, then." Relieved he wouldn't be losing his valet, Lord David scanned the papers on his desk. Before he selected one, however, he looked up again. "Is it . . . bad?"

Westing's grimace spoke volumes. After a moment, he schooled his features into a braver expression. "'Tis worth it."

"Let us hope so," Lord David murmured. He cleared his throat and turned back to sifting through more businesses to approach. He picked up the profile of the city's new silk filature. Doctor Franklin himself had helped to start the silk industry in the environs.

Lord David hadn't found a suitable silk to send to Cassandra Crofton yet, and Dr. Rush had just charged him to stay in. Ah well, she'd like the gift as well once he was recovered.

He looked back to the business profiles. They'd widened the net in the last few days. Although several of these businesses did not appear as lucrative as the first batch of prospects, several of them severely needed help. Westing helped him sort those into a pile all their own and stack them neatly on the corner of his desk. He didn't dare meet with the owners while he was in the inoculation process, but perhaps it was a start.

Cassandra jolted awake when the coach came to a stop. The ride over the rutted streets outside of town and the pebbled street within the city limits was anything but comfortable, but the warmth of the afternoon and simply being off her feet had lulled her to sleep.

She tapped Helen's knee, waking her as well, and they dragged themselves into the house. The Kaufmann family had been terribly grateful for their help, and their little girls had been much more comfortable by the time they'd left.

Still, it didn't feel as though they'd done enough when they knew ten other houses had the smallpox, not including their own cousins.

When they walked in, Temperance sprang up from the couch, exaggeratedly motioning for them to keep quiet. "You're back," she exclaimed in a whisper. "Mama is sleeping."

"Ah." They both glanced at the green paneled ceiling, as if they could see their aunt up there.

"You must be exhausted. Did you sleep there?"

"Some," Cassandra said, though the answer was closer to *very little*.

"And you must be hungry. We have bread and leftover beef on the table."

"How are Verity and Mercy?" Helen asked.

"Sleeping as well." Temperance's murmur betrayed her resignation. Two weeks after they'd begun the inoculation, the girls had both taken sick. That was good—desirable, even—but keeping them comfortable without overtaxing their mother had required all three of the older sisters, and frequently Helen and Cassandra, if they were home.

Temperance looked at the two of them. "You should get some rest as well. After you eat." She gestured to the kitchen.

Helen sighed, a deep, bone-weary sigh. "I think I shall rest first."

Cassandra caught her sister's hand and then her gaze, silently checking to make sure she was well. Helen offered a smile that seemed only weakened by lack of sleep and patted her fingers, so Cassandra let her go.

Temperance led Cassandra to the dining room, and Constance got up with her mending to join them. Patience remained in her chair, poring over a book.

"She could read law at the rate she goes," Constance murmured. Cassandra wasn't sure whether her tone was meant to be impressed or disdainful.

"She would love that." Temperance was clearly on the impressed side. "Besides, I know you're not teasing anyone for reading."

Constance blushed a little, hiding her ink-stained fingers. "That's not the same."

Temperance dished up a plate for Cassandra and settled across the table from her. "How are the children?" Temperance asked.

"How did you know there were children?"

"Every family you've helped has children. I think you have a soft spot."

Cassandra laughed softly and tucked a stray strand of hair back under her lace cap. "Perhaps so. Two children today. They are quite ill."

Temperance frowned in sympathy, casting her eyes toward the ceiling again. "It's so warm," she lamented. "I wish we could have done this in April so they could have the cold air they need."

"The rags seem to be helping," Constance assured her sister. She tied the final knot in sewing the patch beneath one arm of a blue striped cotton gown and switched to the second sleeve. Both of the sisters' usually mercurial natures were much subdued, but then, when there was sickness in the house, it was hard to be as buoyant as they normally were.

"I don't know how you do it," Constance said.

It was a moment before Cassandra realized her cousin was addressing her. "Do what?"

"Help those people. I love my sisters, and I would do anything for them, but I can't imagine helping someone else that way, especially if I had just come from an estate—"

Temperance waved her off. "Hush."

"I don't mean anything ill, it's simply—it's hard work. You know that."

Cassandra couldn't disagree. It was hard work, every minute. And no, a year ago, she couldn't have imagined doing this, let alone feeling so ... fulfilled by it. "It is hard, but it's good work," she concluded aloud.

They had started with Ginny's cousins, and now they went wherever they were needed in Germantown. They even slept there occasionally when the children they were helping were very sick, as they had been last night. They tried to feed them broth, to ease their fevers, to keep them from picking at the pox and to occupy their minds, giving their parents a few minutes' peace. Three times, she'd held the children's arms for bloodletting, which she'd never believed she could have done. The first children they'd helped were already beginning to recover.

The front door opened, and all three women turned toward the sound.

"Papa?" came Patience's voice from the drawing room. "Did you walk home?"

"Yes. How are the little girls?"

"Sleeping."

"And your mother?" The note of urgency in Uncle Josiah's voice was new to Cassandra.

"Also asleep."

Footsteps approached the dining room, and Cassandra turned with her cousins to wait for Uncle Josiah to appear. Patience trailed after him.

"Oh, Cassandra, you're home. Where is Helen?"

"She's just gone up to sleep. It was a long night."

Uncle Josiah pressed his lips together, grim.

"What are you doing home, Papa?" Temperance asked.

His mouth worked a moment before any words worked their way out. Cassandra had never seen her uncle speechless.

"It's Lord David," he concluded. "His valet has taken sick—

not the smallpox—and he has no one to nurse him."

The four women in the room studied one another. Uncle Josiah had stopped short of asking them, but could any of them refuse Lord David? Surely Temperance and Constance would leap at the "romantic" opportunity to nurse a nobleman back to health.

Instead, Cassandra found that all the eyes in the room were now upon her. "Surely not?" She'd just returned from nursing half a dozen strangers. Why on earth would she run to help a man who hated her, and with good reason?

"I'm tending Verity," Temperance said.

"And I Mercy," Patience said.

"Mama," Constance said. "And Helen."

Cassandra felt every gaze settle on her again. "Have you brought a doctor? Has he been bled?"

"Yes, this morning. I'm afraid to try again."

The weight of their gazes still rested on her shoulders. Was this really her responsibility? After the way he'd treated her?

After the way *she* had treated *him*, perhaps she should take any opportunity to make amends.

"Cassandra," Uncle Josiah said, his voice gentler. "I know you've worked so hard with the Germans. I know I can trust him to your care."

Uncle Josiah had confidence in her? Somehow, that meant more than anything.

"Fine, I'll go." She shoved two more bites of beef into her mouth, checked her working jacket and petticoat—clean enough—and took a slice of bread.

Temperance fetched fresh rags for her basket. Constance wrapped up the rest of sliced bread, leaving the loaf. Patience brought over a bottle, stuffing in a cork. "Beef broth," she said, tucking it alongside the bread and rags. "I'll warm more for the girls."

Cassandra thanked each of them and turned to leave. Uncle Josiah stood there, beaming at her with pride shining in his eyes. "Thank *you*," he said.

Chapter 9

*I*t was terribly unfitting for a gentleman's daughter to eat
on her way to the coach. It was terribly unfitting for a
gentleman's daughter to run about in working clothes. It
was terribly unfitting for a gentleman's daughter to never once
check a mirror to set the rest of her hair to rights.

And most likely, it was terribly unfitting for a gentleman's
daughter—or anyone else's daughter—to nurse a man who was
not a member of her family.

Cassandra didn't particularly care.

Her suspicions about propriety seemed confirmed when
Uncle Josiah ordered the coach to pull to the back alley behind
his law office. He directed her to the stairs up to the apartment
above, making sure she was unseen.

"I'll be right below you if you need anything." He searched
her face, making sure his meaning was clear.

"Thank you." She'd witnessed firsthand how weak the
disease and even the inoculation could make one, so she
wasn't terribly worried Lord David would be a threat to her
person.

Uncle Josiah handed her the key, and she stole up the alley stairs. She knocked before she entered, but there was no response. She didn't bother to check the study, the only other room she'd visited before. The other doors off the hall led to a dining room and a drawing room, all furnished with modest necessities. The last door led to a bedroom dominated by a large but plain bed and an oppressive heat.

The sparse accommodations were probably not what Lord David was used to, but there he was under the coverlet. His cheeks were flushed, but the rest of his face was pale beneath dark stubble.

She closed the door behind her, and he stirred. He focused on her, blinking for a moment. "Is this a dream?"

"Do you often dream of me?" Cassandra asked.

"Don't dream of anything right now." He closed his eyes and seemed to sink deeper into the pillows, though he hadn't sat up in the first place.

She crossed the room. "How are you?"

He opened his eyes again, still languid. "Wonderful. I think I shall go to the Royal Governor's ball tonight."

"You'll be the toast of the town." If that was not a joke, she had better check his fever. She reached for his forehead but pulled back. "May I?"

He squinted at her. "May you what?"

She'd hoped after his joke that he was a little more lucid than that. "May I touch you?"

Lord David's eyelids drifted closed. "Why are you here?"

"Uncle Josiah said you needed a nurse, that your valet was ill."

"I don't need a nursemaid."

"You're in luck; I'm not a nursemaid."

He groaned in response, and Cassandra finally pressed her fingertips to his forehead. Burning hot.

"Why are your windows closed?" she asked.

"I'm perfectly frozen, aren't you?"

She checked the temperature of his neck, equally hot and clammy. "That's the fever talking."

"Westing says it does that. I do that."

"Then today shall be entertaining." Cassandra was already across the room, throwing open the sashes. She was relieved the windows opened on the alley and that the alley stood vacant. "Have you eaten?"

Lord David vaguely shook his head and his shoulders twitched. She'd take that for a no. The beef broth Temperance had given her was still warm. After a quick search, she found a bowl and spoon in the kitchen and poured in the contents of the bottle.

When she returned to the room, already the oppressive heat had lessened. She set the bowl on the night table. "Let's sit up."

"What?"

Cassandra had to kneel on the bed and use both hands and all her weight to pull him forward enough to wedge another pillow behind him. His head was a bit more elevated now, enough to drink broth at least. "Let's get some broth in you."

"Where did—" He paused to grimace. "Where did a gentleman's daughter learn to nurse the sick?"

"By nursing the sick. With my mother." She retrieved the bowl and settled herself on the bed facing him. "Open up."

Lord David obeyed and swallowed five spoonfuls of soup before he spoke again. "I don't deserve your kindness."

"I think you have that backwards."

"Who is feeding whom?"

Cassandra smiled. She painstakingly spooned the rest of the broth between his lips. A little of his natural color had returned by the time he finished the bowl. She checked his forehead again, still very hot.

She returned the empty bowl to the kitchen. She hoped the water in the bucket on the sideboard was fresh enough. It smelled fine and seemed clean once she ladled it into a laver. She took that back to the night table and threw in the rags Temperance had given her.

"You needn't do this," Lord David said.

"I know." Cassandra wrung out one of the rags and laid it across his forehead, then wrapped a second around the back of his neck.

"Am I a good patient?"

"I don't know yet. Before now I would have said you were quite *im*patient." She wasn't here to insult him further. "At times," she added, though she doubted it did much to soften the blow. "Do you think you can eat now?"

"No."

"Then I'll let you rest for a while." She started from the room.

"Stay?"

She turned back. "Was that a command or a question?"

"A question. It's very ... quiet."

Cassandra hesitated a moment. She hadn't come here to spend time with the poor man, but that sounded very lonely. She dragged a striped side chair over to sit by the bed. For once, she wished she did know how to knit.

She should try to take his mind off his suffering, as she did with the children. Though she doubted her somewhat embellished stories of a grand house on a grand estate in grand Surrey would be half so grand to Lord David.

"I should be used to the quiet," he murmured. "But I hate it."

"Was your home in England quiet?"

"Yes. My brothers were away at school by the time I was

old enough to be of any interest to them."

"You have only brothers?"

Lord David grimaced. "I had a sister. Georgette. But she died long before I was born."

"Oh, I'm sorry."

"Smallpox."

No wonder his family had been so cautious of miasmas. How had he consented to the inoculation, then?

It was better than the alternative.

She checked the rags. Already they were warm. She changed them for fresh ones. Unlike so many of the children in Germantown, his face wasn't riddled with pox. Her cousins' pox were concentrated near their incisions as well.

"May I see your pox?" she asked, hoping to occupy his mind that way.

He held out his hand, the most she'd seen him move of his own accord since she'd arrived. She moved closer to pull up the sleeve of his linen nightshirt. A fresh bandage was tied around his elbow from where they must have already bled him. But there was no sign of the cut where they would have placed the thread on his biceps.

"Where is your incision?"

"Back of my hand."

She inspected his hand instead. As with her cousins, the rash that preceded the pustules was concentrated near the incision. She pointed out the rash. "The distemper is progressing."

"Good to hear." He let his sleeve fall again but caught hold of her hand. Cassandra froze as he met her eyes.

"Do you know?" he said. "You're my oldest friend in the colonies."

She gently squeezed his fingertips and released him. "That's the fever talking."

"It isn't."

"Then you've given me an honor I don't deserve." Could he really mean that? What had she ever done to merit his friendship? And would that prove to be a blessing or a curse?

First it would have to prove stronger than the fever.

Lord David held her gaze. "I've known you longer than anyone else here, other than your sister."

"I suppose that's true for me as well."

"Good." He closed his eyes and relaxed into the pillows. "Now we are old friends."

Definitely the illness talking. "Your fever should come down soon."

Actually, the fever was beginning to drop off by this stage with most of the children she'd seen. Perhaps the inoculation worked differently. Though her cousins' fevers had broken.

Or perhaps Lord David had a second illness.

Then she had twice the reason to distract him. "What about your parents? The marquess and the marchioness?"

He didn't open his eyes. "What about them?"

"Surely you saw them when you were growing up?" she teased.

"No." His answer was clipped.

"Oh." This sounded like a subject she shouldn't pursue further.

After a long silence, Lord David spoke again. "What about your parents? The gentleman and the lady."

"Papa could be firm, but he loved us. Made sure we got a good education. Mama taught me everything I know about caring for the sick. She was very charitable and kind."

"Was?"

"They're dead." She paused. This was hardly the topic one discussed when an "old friend" was on his sickbed, but she needed to distract him somehow. "Mama was taken when I was thirteen. Infection. She was Uncle Josiah's younger sister."

"And your father?"

"Cancer. A year ago now."

"I'm sorry."

Cassandra nodded her thanks, although Lord David had yet to look at her again.

"And you and your sister could not inherit?"

"Papa was a life tenant." Due to the way his great-grandfather had established the estate, Papa had only had the right to live at Heartcomb during his lifetime. No matter what he'd wished, nothing was passed to his daughters. Not even an annuity from Cousin Lowell, the miserable... miser.

Cassandra checked the rags on Lord David's forehead and neck. They'd again warmed with the fever, so she switched them out with fresh ones. As she mopped his forehead, his eyes flew open. She'd never realized they were such a remarkable shade of sappShire blue.

"I'll grant you this: you're a better nurse than my valet," he said. "Your mother taught you well."

Was he giving her a compliment? "Thank you."

"Did you say you brought food?"

"Are you feeling well enough to eat?"

"No, but I may not get the chance if you leave. After you leave," he corrected himself.

Cassandra handed him a slice of bread. He tore off the corner and ate it.

Something in her didn't want the conversation to end, though she wasn't certain why. Probably because she was still duty-bound to distract him. Perhaps she could try to cheer him. Didn't the Bible say, "A merry heart doeth good like a medicine"? She steeled herself. "Can I ask you something... impertinent?"

"I shall make a hasty exit to avoid it."

Cassandra checked the room, trying to gauge whether he could actually walk that far, but she realized he was joking. She took that as permission. "How many of your trunks were filled with clothing?"

"What?" He did laugh, once and then again. "Has that been on your mind all this time?"

"Every moment since we left England."

He laughed once more, with more energy, and her heart swelled. Yes, laughter did do good.

"Two and a half," he finally answered. "The other half of that one was shoes and buckles and cufflinks. And four for books."

"Oh." She failed to conceal her surprise.

"Did you really think me that vain? Or that stupid?"

Cassandra opened her mouth to speak but found no words. She settled on closing it again.

"I see." He gave her one final laugh, and for that moment, he seemed to be in the best health he'd been in all day.

"Shall I read to you then?"

"Because I'm so stupid?"

"Of course not. Obviously you didn't bring the books because you thought they'd look nice in your study."

A grin fought past his distemper and defenses.

Cassandra shook her head. "To think how bored I was after reading the only books we had all those weeks."

"Oh, wasn't it awful?"

"It was awful—and you were awful!"

Lord David made a little noise of indignation. "Was I? I seem to remember you being very rude to me."

She lowered her gaze a moment.

"And that food?" he added.

"You call that food?" Her stomach turned at the thought of ever seeing a hard tack biscuit again.

He pressed a hand to his middle. "Never again."

"Fortunately, Polly's bread is much better." She nodded at the bread, forgotten in his other hand. "Shall I read then? While you eat?"

"Perhaps later. Tell me about your estate."

"Heartcomb?"

"Heartcomb," Lord David repeated. He tore off another bite of bread and motioned for her to continue.

Chapter 10

*L*ord David shifted on the pillows Cassandra insisted on stacking behind him at every visit. Was it so wrong to want to lie down?

The fever wasn't even the worst of it. The rash had developed into large, hideous blisters. On top of that, his body still ached. And then there was the fever.

On second thought, the fever *was* the worst of it. He groaned, more in frustration than discomfort.

Cassandra looked up from the book she was reading aloud. Truth be told, he wasn't paying much attention, but he liked to hear her voice. She always managed to maintain kindness in her tone and her eyes, no matter how intractable the illness made him.

Or perhaps he was always intractable.

Cassandra set aside the book. "Why don't we talk a while?"

He had no strength to argue. "If you insist."

"I do. Tell me about Dorset."

"It isn't interesting."

Cassandra settled back in her chair as if he'd proposed a

contest to keep her entertained. He swallowed a sigh. Very well. "In the days of the Romans—"

"Feel free to begin at the present. I am not your governess."

"I daresay you are not." His governess had been a very cruel woman, and he was finally beginning to see that Cassandra was not. Despite the way she'd treated him initially. That same lady couldn't have treated with him such kindness every day for four days. Or was it five?

She was still waiting for him to speak. For a moment, he forgot himself, pondering the remarkable amber color of her eyes.

"Are you well?" she asked.

"Yes—well, no, obviously not." He gestured at his present circumstances.

"Shall I go?"

"No, no—Dorset. Ah, we have a number of villages, farms, estates, weavers—I promise, this is as interesting as it gets."

"Obviously storytelling is not your gift." Cassandra gave him a sarcastic smile.

"Shall I read to you then?" Lord David reached for the book.

She did not offer it to him. "Dorset."

This time he let the sigh escape. "You are impossible." He couldn't entertain her with the three-month-old talk of the ton, what little he remembered. He'd be hard pressed to find some heartwarming memory of his family like the ones she'd shared. What else of more recent history? Dorset had been home to plenty of royalists in the Civil War, although it had also fomented the Monmouth Rebellion and the Glorious Revolution, but all that was a hundred years ago or more. What else had ever happened of consequence there? "There were smugglers."

Cassandra leaned forward, the kindness in her eyes turning

to captivation. "Smugglers?"

"Yes. I was a boy when they hanged the last of them."

She didn't seem disappointed. Rather, she was hanging on his words. "Were they dangerous?"

"Yes, very." This wasn't some romantic privateer's tale; those men had murdered and extorted dozens, perhaps hundreds, of people. And there was nothing romantic about their executions or the gibbet field where the bodies had hung for months afterwards.

He suppressed a shudder and refocused on Cassandra. He wanted to change the topic, but to see her so fascinated—by him?

He didn't dare do anything that might jeopardize that.

"Well," he began. "They were called the Hawkhurst Gang."

Cassandra rushed into the Hayes house. She knew she was too late for dinner, but she hoped Helen hadn't left for Germantown yet.

"Here she is!" Constance called from the couch in a whisper. "Finally."

"How do you do to you, too, cousin? Are the little girls not well?" At twelve and fourteen, Mercy and Verity were not all that little, but Cassandra had fallen into the family's pattern of referring to them that way.

"Merely sleeping. I think they're past the worst."

Cassandra frowned. Lord David was not. He'd seemed extra uncomfortable this morning, until she'd distracted him with talking about an awful gang of smugglers. It would not have been the topic she would have picked—who talked of pirates, murderers and thieves in polite company?—but once he started, she had to own she was enthralled.

Temperance came down the stairs to her right. "Oh, there you are." She acquired a wicked tone. "How is Lord David?"

"Not well."

That did not deter Temperance. "How perfectly scandalous for you to be visiting him in such a state."

A state where he found sitting up taxing? Cassandra didn't dignify her cousin with a reply, at least not to her implication. "He's unwell, and I'm nursing him."

"Perhaps he'll have to marry you once he's well again." Constance looked up from her writing again, a dreamy look on her face. "My cousin, a marchioness."

"His mother is the marchioness. And once his father is gone, his sister-in-law will be."

"Oh, close enough." Constance returned to her scribbling.

"Please," Cassandra said, looking at both of her cousins. "Promise me you won't tell anyone?"

"Upon my word," Temperance exclaimed. "Of course not! Why would we do that to our own cousin? I'd never be able to marry Winthrop Morley if you were ruined."

Ah. Although their discretion was apparently not out of concern for Cassandra herself, she appreciated it.

Helen finally rushed down the stairs, her basket of supplies already on her arm. Patience arrived from the dining room with bread and cheese for Cassandra. She didn't have the heart to tell her she'd taken dinner with Lord David, opting instead to thank her cousin. The poor families they were visiting could surely use the food.

Cassandra refilled her own supply basket, and they hurried out to the coach.

"How was Lord David today?" Helen asked once they were underway. Her voice carried a note of disdain, and Cassandra felt herself bristle a bit.

"His fever hasn't broken yet."

Helen expressed the same concern she had, then she sighed. "I don't know how you put up with that odious man. I couldn't do it."

"He isn't that bad."

Helen snorted. "He wouldn't even deign to speak with us after we spent nine weeks with him in such narrow quarters. He must have heard your snoring."

She scoffed. "You mean *your* snoring."

"I thought I was patient to put up with that din you make." Helen shook her head. "Clearly you are the saint to stand being around him. Don't let him bully you. We know his type. They take a firm hand."

"He really isn't that bad," Cassandra insisted.

Her sister turned to her, ready to argue her point again, as always, but stopped short. "Dearest, are you well?"

"Why?"

"Your cheeks are flushed." Helen felt Cassandra's cheek and forehead. "Wait—you're not blushing, are you?"

"No, of course not."

Helen watched her for a long moment. "What do you think of Lord David?" she asked, obviously testing her.

"He's perfectly fine."

"Is he?" Helen arched an eyebrow. "Laying aside the fact that you just said he's unwell, you used to hate him more than I did. What on earth changed your mind?"

"I haven't—but I know him better now."

"Hm." Helen studied her for a long minute before Cassandra angled her face away. To look out the window.

Or to hide another blush she could feel stealing over her face.

"It's all right," Helen said gently. "I haven't sworn an oath to hate him as a villain until the end of my days. I mean, not one I couldn't undo."

Cassandra laughed. "I—he's just—he's my friend." She suddenly remembered how he'd taken her hand the first time she'd gone to care for him, gently, and said she was his oldest friend in the colonies. The oldest friend he had now.

Her cheeks burned even hotter.

She must have been embarrassed because she'd treated him so poorly. Or because she'd changed her mind about him. Or because he'd proven her wrong.

She snuck a peek at her sister. Helen said nothing, her eyes on the window.

But the secretive mirth on her sister's face seemed to say she already knew everything.

Even the parts Cassandra refused to think.

The fever was not supposed to persist this long. Lord David had suspected as much, but when Josiah brought Dr. Rush to see him again, he confirmed the suspicion. "You may have a second illness," the doctor informed him.

How lucky.

"Hopefully not yellow fever."

Or perhaps not.

"I want you up and walking as soon as possible," Dr. Rush said. "I know it sounds singular, but in my experience, it consistently leads to an easy progress of the disease. For now, we had better bleed you."

Hadn't he been bled yesterday?

"Fine." It was all he could do to focus on the man, but he recognized his look. It was the look of someone losing a battle. If Lord David had any strength left, he should have been frightened that he was the one about to be lost.

He barely flinched when the doctor sliced his arm. Was this the second or third time he'd been let with this fever? Or more? He couldn't be certain anymore. Even the days and the nights blended together.

The only thing he had to mark time were visits from Cassandra Crofton. Westing had recovered, but she still came to check on him and make sure he was receiving proper care.

She'd just been there that morning. Afternoon. Yesterday? He wasn't sure, but he didn't think he had anything to look forward to.

The next time he opened his eyes, his elbow was bandaged, and Cassandra was sitting in the chair beside his bed. He needed her kindness today more than ever.

A gentleman's daughter ought to have something to keep her hands busy, needlework or some such, because Cassandra's were wringing one another in her lap.

"How do you feel?" she asked.

"Excellent. Clearly the Philadelphia climate agrees with me."

She offered a weak smile, then gestured at his hand. "The sores are progressing."

The sores were even more revolting than they'd seemed on other people, but at least there were fewer of them then there would have been otherwise.

"Would you care for a damp rag? Cool water? Cider?"

Lord David turned his head away, the most he could move.

Cassandra took his hand, which she rarely did. "Come along, Uncle Josiah tells me Dr. Rush wants you walking."

He swatted her hand away.

"Lord David, don't be a child."

"I'm not being a child."

"Oh? Because it certainly looks as though you're behaving

like a spoiled child. Or perhaps that's because you were one?"

Her tone held teasing, but her words held a toxin. He'd never wanted for anything materially, true, but he had been far from coddled.

"I've already had two children die in my arms this week." Now her voice was solid metal. "I'll not lose another."

He was not a child. He turned back to her.

"Get up," she commanded him.

There was no kindness in her eyes today. No respect either.

He knew that expression. More than sympathy, more than pain, somehow sadder than the one he'd seen from Dr. Rush and Westing and Josiah, but she'd never looked at him this way. In the hours she'd spent here, she'd talked with him and laughed with him and read to him, but she'd never looked at him this way. In the weeks—no, months—he'd known her, she had been rude and haughty and snide—and kind—but she'd never looked at him this way.

Today her amber eyes held pity. Contemptuous pity.

He blinked slowly, trying to make sure he was seeing this correctly. But he already knew that scorn far too well to mistake it. How many times had others—his own family—regarded him that way?

As if he were nothing, less than nothing, a sorry waste of a life?

He had had more than enough of that disdain. He didn't have to take it, especially not from her.

Heat began to build in his chest, and this time not from the fever. How dare she? She, the daughter of some obscure country squire? Run out of her home and thrust onto the charity of unknown relatives? Who was Miss Cassandra Crofton to sneer at him with contempt?

"Leave me."

She did not react for a long moment. "Beg pardon? Do you want me to get you something?"

"I want you to leave."

Slowly, confusion overtook her features. "Leave? But you're ill—"

"Thank you so much for telling me. I'd never have reached such a conclusion without your astonishing ability to observe the obvious."

Her eyebrows knitted together. "Lord David, the fever is making you delirious."

"I assure you I am in my right mind about this, Miss Crofton."

Now the confusion and the pity warred in her eyes, but the pity won out. "I want to help you."

"Help me?" He'd let her treat him as an equal, and this was where it had gotten him. Perhaps she was right to pity him. Perhaps he was nothing. Perhaps he didn't have a purpose to his life. Perhaps he was going to die in this poxy place.

But he would never die with some lowly gentleman's daughter looking down her nose at him. He struggled to sit up, and Cassandra moved to help him.

He pulled away from her reach. "Do I not make myself clear?" He wished his voice conveyed the fire he felt instead of the fever. "Get out, and do not return."

Cassandra drew back. "You're—are you—do you mean to dismiss me?"

"Yes, girl. Out." He jerked his chin toward the door.

She jerked back as if he'd slapped her. She stood in stunned silence, gaping for six long seconds. And then she snapped her mouth shut, offered him the curtest nod, and spun on her heel. The door snapped shut behind her and her footsteps retreated away.

There was no mistaking the flame behind her countenance. He'd ignited that ember enough times to recognize it, and this time he'd added kindling and a bellows.

He sank back against the pillows, the silence settling uneasily around him.

He'd cast out his oldest friend. His only friend.

Perhaps he deserved whatever happened to him.

Chapter 11

Three days after Lord David had so discourteously dismissed her, Cassandra was still seething. "Who *does* he think he is, really?" she asked Helen as they bobbed along in the coach toward Germantown.

"We knew who he was all along," Helen pointed out.

Cassandra stared out the window at the neat row of brick buildings. That was her sister's version of sympathy. "What sort of position did he think he was in, throwing me out like that?"

"At least he didn't have his valet bodily kick you out."

"And what did I ever do?" If Helen was going to insist on being so unhelpful, Cassandra would simply ignore her comments. The tactics had served them both well enough. "I only risked my reputation to nurse him, take care of him."

"Luckily, no one knows about that, unless you'd like to announce it to the rest of Philadelphia." Helen gestured out the window.

"Yes, but if they did, I should be ruined."

Helen had to concede that point. "Fortunately, Uncle

Josiah's apprentices are quite discreet, he says. If they even noticed."

"Very fortunate." Cassandra sat back hard against the seat. "Think of all the children I could have helped in that time."

"None of whom died for lack of your care."

They knew of four children who had died in the last week, not including the two she'd held. At least he hadn't caused that. But there were plenty of other things she could blame him for. "Can you believe how he treated us all the way across the sea, and then he wants to claim I'm his oldest friend in the colonies, and then tear that all away?"

Helen didn't respond for a long moment, so Cassandra checked her reaction. Rather than finding her incensed or ignoring her, she found Helen's eyes narrowed and her lips pursed, looking . . . perplexed. "He said what?"

"Get out?"

"No, not that. He said you were his oldest friend in the colonies?"

"Oh. Yes." Had she not mentioned that to Helen?

No, she hadn't. Partly because she knew it had to be the fever talking.

And partly because somehow, a part of her truly wished it wasn't.

"What did he mean by that?"

"Merely that I—we—are the only two people he knows here that he met before landing at the docks."

"Yes, but surely he knows someone else who has come to the colonies."

Cassandra sighed. She actually wanted her sister to validate her hopes, say that Lord David had said such a thing especially about her, but here was Helen, attempting to debate the facts of his claim.

Helen turned to her sister. "Wouldn't you rather be shut of

him?"

"Of course."

She'd hesitated for only a sliver of a second, but it was long enough for her sister to catch. Helen's expression grew quizzical. "Surely you don't still ... fancy him?"

"Who? Lord David? That pompous, arrogant—no." She proclaimed it and folded her hands in her lap. "No."

"Apologies," Helen said. She let the conversation settle a moment, but when she spoke again, her voice carried a tone that was deceptively light. "Then you would not care if he did succumb to the smallpox?"

Cassandra swallowed hard. He was very ill, but that wasn't a possibility. Was it? "As a Christian, I should not wish him harm."

"Ah. I'd forgotten you were so very devout."

"Quite." Obviously even after sixteen years, she would never escape her sister's teasing about the solid year she'd thrown a fit over going to church. Today, she'd take it if it meant deflecting the conversation away from that topic.

Helen rode in silence for two blocks. "He *is* handsome."

"Who?" She feigned ignorance. "Our Lord?"

"*Your* lord."

Cassandra skewered her sister with a scowl. "I do not appreciate you making a joke of our Savior that way."

"I—you—" Helen rolled her eyes heavenward and pressed her palms together. "Forgive me."

Cassandra wasn't sure how her sister could both mock her and be perfectly pious to God at the exact same time.

She and her sister swayed side by side as the coach rode on. She was glad that she had all her time back so she could help her family and the needy. Lord David had no need of her help anymore.

Except that he obviously had needed her that day. He was

so pale and listless, and even though she could do little but try to make him comfortable, her heart had ached to help him.

If she was honest, it still did.

No. She could not own to even knowing a man who would treat her with so little respect. After she'd told him about her parents, Heartcomb, so many things that were so personal to her. And he'd shared his own stories, when he'd had the strength.

That hadn't been enough, in the end. He'd always see her as a dowdy little country bumpkin, hardly fit to make his acquaintance. If her reputation had been ruined, he would never have lowered himself to do the honorable thing.

But marrying him was the last thing she wanted.

She held a hand to her chest to try to relieve the hollow ache.

They *had* shared personal things. She was beginning to believe that they *were* friends. And then for him to treat her with such contempt? What had she done to deserve that?

Perhaps it was the fever talking. Or perhaps the fever had only allowed him to show his true nature, the way he truly felt about her. That he had never respected her. Could never respect her.

"Well, fortunately, we shall never have to see Lord David again," Helen concluded.

"Indeed."

Although he did live above Uncle Josiah's law office, certainly she could avoid him. It wasn't as though they would associate in the same society.

Why did that thought not bring her any comfort?

The fever had finally begun to subside by the time Lord David's first letter from his family arrived. He had to read it three times to be sure he understood everything his mother was saying.

Actually, it wasn't what she was saying that was difficult to comprehend. It was what she hadn't said that boggled the mind, as recently fever-addled as it was.

After the salutation, there was literally no mention of him. No questions. No messages from anyone to pass along—and it wasn't as though he'd been entirely friendless. The closest she came to mentioning him was sharing the latest gossip about Miss Arabella Simpson, whom she had not-very-subtly tried to push on him for the last two years.

He checked every inch of both pages and there was nothing more personal to be found than a story of his niece—clever, but spiteful, very like someone he knew. His mother could have sent this letter to literally anyone in their circle of acquaintance. Anyone to whom she was willing to show how big of a gossip she was, anyway.

Lord David tossed the letter away and it landed on the coverlet. Even thousands of miles away, his family didn't notice he was gone. Didn't care.

He shouldn't have been surprised. They'd hardly attended him when he lived under the same roof.

He looked back at the letter. At least she had thought to write, hadn't she? Shouldn't he be grateful she hadn't forgotten him the moment he was out of sight?

Lord David thrust the thought from his mind. He'd spent too much of his life living under their contempt. No, he wasn't Georgette, and he could never replace her, but did that mean they had to hate him so?

He rubbed at the scabs along his wrist, trying not to damage the skin. Had his mother even cared about keeping him from the smallpox? Or had she only kept him away from miasmas because she wished she could have protected Georgette?

Clearly he could not simply *not* think of this. He reached for the book on his night table, *Robinson Crusoe*.

Cassandra had read to him from that book.

Of course, she'd also regarded him with that same contempt he'd felt his whole life. He didn't have to be treated that way any longer. He wouldn't stand for it.

Hadn't she?

Lord David opened the book to the correct page where she'd left off.

Why had her scorn bothered him so? Shouldn't he have been used to that treatment by now?

Not from her. Cassandra had been . . . respectful.

Perhaps that wasn't the right word. At least she'd treated him like a person.

And he'd treated her as less than human.

She'd been more than respectful to him. She'd been kind. That was something he'd never received from Arabella Simpson or anyone else in their set, and especially not his family.

And that must have been why it stung so badly to lose it for that moment.

A moment that he might have misinterpreted.

A moment that he might have well made permanent.

Lord David set the book aside on the bed. It landed on top of the letter. That blasted letter. As soon as he had the strength to get to the fireplace, he'd burn it.

Why on earth did he care so much about what his family thought? They'd shown how little they cared for him already, abundantly. Why did he ever care about his worth to them?

He sank back against the pillow. What *was* his worth? If he wasn't Lord David Beaufort, youngest son of the Marquess of Dorset, youngest brother of the Earl of Somerset, who in all of the British Empire would have ever cared to have known him?

Not Arabella Simpson.

And at this point, probably not Cassandra Crofton, either.

He deserved that. He'd been so focused on her pity that it became all he could see. Why shouldn't she pity him? Who didn't look pitiful under the effects of a fever?

And then he forgot who she was and how much he cared about her—and treated her the exact same way his family had always treated him.

Who cared who her father was? Who cared who *his* father was?

That was not what mattered. That was not why he'd left. That was not why he'd come here. He'd come here for purpose.

Cassandra had found hers in helping the less fortunate, the sick families of Germantown. Was there some way he could find purpose beyond his father's money and title?

He could try. It would probably not be enough to show that he understood how wrong he'd been to Cassandra, but for his own sake, he had to try.

Had he really thought he could buy her favor with a few lengths of silk? He could buy the entire silk filature and present it to her, and still he wouldn't deserve her notice.

He rang the bell for Westing, who appeared quickly. "Yes, sir?"

"Let's get dressed."

"Dressed?"

Lord David forgave him his surprise. It had been at least three weeks since he'd had the strength to get out of bed, despite Dr. Rush's repeated orders. "Yes, dressed. I have work to do."

"You have?"

Lord David threw aside the covers and threw his feet over the side of the bed. He let Westing help him to his feet. Once standing, he was mostly steady. "Dr. Rush wanted me up and walking," he said. "So up and walking I must be."

"Naturally, sir. I'll get your clothing."

Ten minutes later, he was dressed to the waistcoat and in his study. He still desperately needed a shave, but already he was beginning to feel better. Possibly simply because he was doing something.

The papers on his desk were still laid out in the piles where he'd left them. As he'd widened the net in the search, he'd found a number of slightly riskier investments, ones that might not yield the same level of return, but ones where the owners clearly needed the help. They seemed to be honest workers, based on the profiles Josiah had sent up, but he hadn't met them himself.

Perhaps Westing could visit them to ascertain whom he could help the most. Yes, that seemed wise, especially in his current state.

Ignoring the scabs on his hands and wrists, he began a list of the establishments Westing should visit. This was precisely what he needed.

Or nearly so.

The days and weeks had already run together for Cassandra. She wasn't exactly sure the time of day in this cramped, dark cabin. The smallpox outbreak in Germantown had only gotten worse, while her cousins were almost completely healed. Clearly, the inoculation was a far superior method than suffering through the full illness as she and Helen had done years ago.

Helen finished preparing an oatmeal plaster, and Cassandra applied the plaster to her little patient's stomach. The girl didn't speak a word of English—didn't even understand when they asked her name—but she'd made it obvious that the itching from the scabs was unbearable. At least she was nearly healed. The last three families they'd seen today all had at least one child who looked like they wouldn't make it through the night.

They'd brought food to families who were too weak to feed themselves, tried to soothe the aches and fevers, applied plasters for healing, and even cleaned up sick, which Cassandra was fairly certain should qualify her to be awarded the Order of the Bath. It had certainly qualified her for a bath, at the least.

Once she'd been so thoroughly dismissed by Lord David, Cassandra had had more time to help the families of Germantown. So it was for the best. Even if she actually missed sitting and talking with him, reminiscing about home and some of the more ridiculous people they'd known. She'd thought they were friends, or even equals.

She'd been wrong.

The little girl's whimpering finally quieted, and Cassandra checked on the next child. The little boy lay still—too still. Cassandra touched his hand, trying to find a patch of skin that wasn't covered with the sores.

He was cold.

Cassandra shook him, but he remained limp.

"Helen," she whispered. "He's gone."

Helen looked over at him, and her shoulders sank, like Cassandra's heart did. The children's mother was still feverish, but the father had already survived the smallpox. Helen caught his attention and directed him to his son.

Without a word, the man gathered him up into his arms and proceeded to weep.

Helen and Cassandra quietly collected their things and slipped out.

That had definitely been the hardest part of the past weeks: the children who didn't make it. Sometimes, the meaning she'd found in nursing the sick was cold comfort.

Cassandra was surprised to find the sky darkening already. Uncle Josiah's coach would be waiting. Helen took her free hand as they walked to where they were to meet the coach. "We did all that we could for them."

Cassandra agreed, although she couldn't help but wonder if they'd arrived sooner, or if they'd come to this house yesterday, if the little boy might still have been alive.

Of course, there was little they could do to stop the disease. They didn't have medicine or training. All they had was the example of their mother to follow, and Cassandra had only seen that in person a few times. She'd mostly heeded Helen's directions, since she'd gone out with Mama more.

Helen seemed to read her mind—or she was following the same line of thought. "Mama always said that every kindness we can offer is enough. We're doing all we can."

Cassandra nodded. Her mind knew that there was nothing more they could have done, and they were lucky they could help anyone in the family. But her heart wished otherwise. From Helen's tone, she could tell her sister felt the same.

They reached the coach and went to open the door, but it opened before they could touch it, and Uncle Josiah leaned out to lend them a hand. "Good evening, nieces."

This was a surprise. "Good evening," they greeted him. He helped each of them into the coach and bid the driver to proceed toward home.

"Look at my ladies," Uncle Josiah mused.

Indeed, they hardly looked like ladies now. Cassandra didn't want to think of the amount of filth caked on her petticoats—nor the number of things she'd done in the last few weeks that no one of breeding could have imagined.

"What brings you out to Germantown?" Helen asked the question that was on both of their minds. What could be so important that he couldn't wait until they returned home for supper?

"I just had an exciting conversation, and I wanted you two to be the first who heard."

Cassandra and Helen exchanged a mystified glance. Whom had he spoken to?

Perhaps . . . Lord David?

"I don't suppose either of you know Dr. Drinker, do you?"

They shook their heads in unison. There wasn't much use for doctors in Germantown. Aside from not sharing a language, there was little a doctor could do that they weren't already doing. Tinctures and plasters notwithstanding, the smallpox simply had to run its course. Unless they wanted to bleed the patients. That was obviously beyond their expertise.

"Well, I mentioned how you'd been helping in Germantown, and he was most intrigued. He said he had been wanting for an assistant to help with calls."

"As in a nurse?" Helen asked.

Uncle Josiah nodded.

"As a permanent position?" Cassandra asked.

"Quite possibly."

No one did such a thing, but if she could continue helping people once the smallpox outbreak had finished its course? That was the best news she'd had in days. Probably since she'd been unceremoniously discharged by Lord David.

"Not me, I'm afraid," Helen said quickly. "If there's one

thing I've learned, it's that you're much better suited to this, dearest." Helen squeezed her hand.

"Thank you." At least, she thought it was a compliment. She could certainly understand why one wouldn't choose this type of work, but it felt good to be useful.

It was an altogether new feeling. They'd amassed such a reputation around Germantown that families who a few weeks ago would never have trusted them now welcomed their help with open arms.

"I understand, Helen," Uncle Josiah said. "You have worked hard, but I know this is not where your heart lies. Know that I'm very proud of you both," Uncle Josiah said. His serene confidence seemed to convey that even more. "No matter what you choose."

"Thank you," they both said.

Cassandra silently consulted her sister. Choosing the same route would obviously be wise. They hadn't undertaken this charity work with the intention of making it into a vocation.

She could walk away from watching children die and go back to a comfortable life as a gentleman's daughter, or at least a successful lawyer's niece, and be perfectly happy.

Well, not perfectly happy.

To be honest, though, the idea of returning to the comfortable life she'd always known held so much less value when compared to pursuing what had come to feel like her calling.

"I would like to work with Dr. Drinker," she finally said.

Uncle Josiah smiled at her. "I'm especially pleased that you might pursue such a singular opportunity, Cassandra." In the silence between his words, Cassandra saw something she hardly recognized in his countenance: esteem. Not the kind of respect one received by virtue of one's birth, but the kind of honor that could only be earned through sincere effort. "Puts me in mind of Elizabeth," he finally finished.

She reminded him of Mama? "Thank you," she said again.

"You know," Uncle Josiah continued, "I was a little concerned when we first brought you home."

Cassandra snuck a peek at her sister, who wore a smile of amusement. "Oh?"

"Well, you were dressed so finely, and clearly had the manners of . . . of someone raised in your circles."

Again, mentioning their birth. Had they not moved past that? Or worse, had they made Uncle Josiah feel awkward? She hoped not.

"And then when you came to dinner that first day in your plainest gowns, I was worried you were . . . mocking us."

"Oh, we're so sorry," Helen said quickly. "We never intended—"

"I see that now. Actually, with the way you treated Lord David, Cassandra, I guessed fairly quickly you wouldn't have stooped to subtler means of mockery."

She pressed a hand to her cheek to hide her blush. She'd been fairly awful to him.

And now it took all her restraint not to ask Uncle Josiah if he'd spoken to Lord David and ask how he was faring. She'd gathered that the smallpox hadn't claimed him—at least she would have expected her uncle to mention that—but she had no idea if he'd recovered.

It shouldn't matter to her. It didn't. He was a spiteful, proud popinjay, and he had been from the moment they'd met.

Helen did her the favor. "Has he recovered?" she asked.

"I believe he has," Uncle Josiah said. He gave Cassandra a quizzical look, and she turned away, as if Helen required her attention at the moment. Lord David certainly didn't.

She needed to forget him. Plain and simple.

And she would. Soon.

Working with the Germans and hopefully Dr. Drinker could only help. Pursuing her vocation would heal more than just the sick.

Or at least it would soon. She hoped.

Chapter 12

Lord David paced across his study from one tall bookcase to the other. He finally had the strength for the walking remedy Dr. Rush had recommended all along, but by now all he had left of the illness was new scars on his hands and wrists.

Still, it was worth it if it meant that he would be safe from the smallpox for the rest of his life. If the inoculation hadn't taken, he might have to endure the whole process over again.

Did the idea of inoculation scare his mother, or would even that not be enough to roust her to care?

That was uncharitable of him, perhaps. Or perhaps it was accurate.

Westing stepped in to announce Josiah Hayes. It was his landlord's first visit since he'd fully recovered, and Lord David could not remember the last time he'd been so eager to see a guest.

Well, he could, but he certainly wouldn't expect her to call again.

"Lord David," Josiah greeted him warmly. "So good to see

you looking well."

"Thank you. Good to see you too." Lord David gestured for them to sit on either side of his desk and miraculously managed not to ask after Cassandra right away.

"Well, how go your business ventures?"

Lord David frowned. "I've really been working to understand the businesses you've recommended, but I'm afraid I still can't decide what to do."

"Ah. What have you tried?"

He furrowed his brow. "Sorry?"

"What have you done as you've tried to understand?"

Oh. Lord David sat up, gesturing at the papers strewn across his desk. "I've had Westing go out and visit the various businesses, talk to the owners, and write up reports on how they're faring."

"That's a good start."

Start? He'd hoped it would be enough to finish.

Clearly he didn't know enough about business to attempt this on his own. Fortunately, he was talking with a man who'd helped businesses for twenty years. "What more must I do?" he asked.

"Well, if you can't understand a business's character from reading about it, perhaps it's time to actually visit the business."

What? But these were grocers and weavers—tradesmen and merchants. He had never—he didn't—he couldn't—

Josiah continued to regard him with his usual equanimity, but a slight spark in his eyes seemed to show he knew how much that was asking of Lord David.

"Why is that so necessary?" he finally managed.

"I find that it helps with my law clients when I visit with them and get to know them. Building that relationship helps me to understand and advocate for them better."

"Ah, interesting." Lord David concentrated on his desk for

a moment. Josiah did make a compelling argument, but . . . Josiah was a man raising five daughters in a single small house. Clearly their family was filled with affection and respect.

Creating personal connection simply was not part of Lord David's world. "I'm afraid that isn't something the nobility are known for."

Josiah accepted his argument. "You must consider your purpose, naturally. If this doesn't suit, you'll find another way."

There it was again: his purpose. Was that personal connection so vital?

He obviously lacked all talent in that area. It had not been a fortnight since he'd severed what was his longest standing friendship in the entire continent over a perception he was not even certain was entirely accurate anymore. "I shall think on it, thank you. How is your family?"

"Well. My younger daughters are recovered from their inoculation, though it seems they took it a bit easier than did you."

"I should hope they did." Lord David swallowed and tried to feign disinterest. "And your nieces? How are they adjusting to life in the colonies?"

"Surprisingly well." Pride shone in Josiah's eyes. "May I confide in you?"

Lord David looked up, touched that the man who was becoming his mentor would want that confidence in him. "To be sure."

"When my nieces arrived—even before they arrived—I was quite concerned that living here would be difficult. Any city is an adjustment compared to a country estate." He paused and nodded to Lord David. "As I'm sure you well know."

Lord David acknowledged his point and gestured for him to continue.

"I was worried they would find our home—our world—

119

very ... narrow. And that was most distressing, because when you disdain something, you seldom learn to appreciate and respect it."

Lord David tried not to shift in his chair. Was this supposed to be a confidence about Cassandra—and her sister—or was this a veiled lecture for him?

"But my nieces." Josiah paused to shake his head in wonder. "They have worked tirelessly to help Germantown through the smallpox. I thought, perhaps, two ladies might be a little more ... overly indulged."

"That is admirable of them," Lord David said. He already knew how talented Cassandra was at easing the pains and discomforts of an illness. It was enough to make a man wish she could always be there.

A wish that was certainly in vain. He would never know such treatment again, not from her. He'd already sealed his own fate.

"I respect the charitable acts that they're doing now so much. I would have taken in my sister's girls no matter what, but it is a singular blessing to have two people who work so hard in the service of others in my household." He glanced around and leaned a little closer. "Some of my daughters can tend toward the ridiculous at times."

"I hadn't noticed." He hoped his smile conveyed the truth: it was impossible to miss that fact, even in his single brief meeting with them.

"Don't mistake me: they are very good girls, and I love each of them dearly. I simply hope they will learn a great deal from their cousins."

"Would that we all had such an excellent exemplar."

"Indeed. You shall have to visit our family again soon." Josiah clapped, signaling he would be taking his leave momentarily. "Well, do you know what you mean to do next?"

Cassandra had been using her talents to help the less fortunate. Could he find a way to do something similar?

Lord David contemplated the papers on his desk. "I think I do. Thank you."

At the worktable in Dr. Drinker's narrow kitchen, Cassandra craned her neck to watch him prepare a mustard plaster. They had only ever prepared oatmeal plasters, so to learn the scientific way of caring for the ill was quite thrilling. It had taken her almost a month to begin this version of an apprenticeship, once the outbreak in Germantown finally seemed more under control.

At last, her life in the colonies seemed to have a future.

Only one thing was lacking.

She pointed to the bowl where he was mixing the mustard seed he'd ground with the pestle. "So you sieve the powder first, you said?" she asked.

"Yes, I find it makes it easier to mix. Must be careful not to leave it on too long, naturally."

"Naturally." Although she already knew the hazards of mustard plasters, Cassandra filed that information away with the rest of the knowledge she'd gained from two days in his tutelage. She wasn't quite sure how that fit with the prevailing cold therapy she'd been taught yesterday: keep the room cool and the patient moving if they are capable. Most of the patients in Germantown weren't able to get up, but her cousins had been ordered to move about a bit as the disease progressed, and that did seem to hasten their recovery.

Was Lord David well enough to move about these days? She hoped so.

"Miss Crofton?" Dr. Drinker addressed her. It must have been the second or third time, judging by the tone of the query. He was patient, and she was striving to learn quickly, but she'd already discovered he didn't appreciate distraction.

"Apologies. You were saying?"

He continued with the explanation of the newest method of inoculation. Cassandra would certainly not be comfortable using that method herself—she was woefully unprepared to wield a lancet. Her cousins had both undergone the method with cuts in each arm and a thread with infection material on it left in the cuts for a few days.

If this new method had rendered Lord David nearly incapacitated, it hardly seemed like a better alternative.

Dr. Drinker took her hand to point out the proper incision site for the new method. She'd seen Lord David's scar closely enough already.

Perhaps it was her imagination, but for a moment, it seemed Dr. Drinker held onto her fingers longer than necessary. She pulled back first. As soon as Dr. Drinker turned away, she watched him for a long moment.

He was young, perhaps not much older than her. With a fine nose and strong jaw, he was certainly handsome.

But he was not Lord David.

Cassandra startled at her own thought. Of course Dr. Drinker wasn't Lord David. Dr. Drinker had done nothing but show her respect and kindness, two things Lord David had only bestowed upon her when he was brought low, nigh unto death. The two men were nothing alike.

And yet her heart still yearned to see Lord David again.

She shook off the thought and refocused on Dr. Drinker's lesson. This was important, vital to her work among the Germantown patients and beyond, she hoped. This had nothing to do with Lord David.

"Well," Dr. Drinker finished. "I believe that's all I'll be able to teach you for today."

Had she gone distracted again? "Apologies. I just... remembered something."

"Well, it's nearly suppertime. I should get you back to your uncle."

"Thank you." Truthfully, it had been a long day, so this distraction hadn't ruined a full day of learning.

Dr. Drinker's home was only two blocks from Uncle Josiah's law office, so Dr. Drinker escorted her to the brick building. She would wait in the office until the coach arrived. She thanked Dr. Drinker at the front steps, but he insisted on escorting her inside. Cassandra couldn't deny him the simple courtesy.

Inside, the office was bustling. Both of the assistants and Uncle Josiah's apprentice were hurriedly rushing from table to table, practically flinging books from one desk to another.

"What about this decision?" one called. "From 1692."

The other two men ran right past Cassandra as if she weren't there. Dr. Drinker took her arm in a protective gesture.

She turned to thank him, but a movement behind him caught her attention: Lord David, descending the stairs from his apartment. He couldn't have been going far without his wig or coat on.

Cassandra wasn't sure whether she should attempt to hide or march up to him and demand the respect he owed her. Fortunately, she was spared having to decide because she was quite rooted to the spot.

Would he be angry to see her here? Did he presume he could banish her from her uncle's office as well?

Or was there some chance he might speak kindly to her?

Lord David took in the chaos with only mild surprise and pivoted to go back upstairs—but he stopped suddenly and turned back to her. "Miss Crofton?"

She bobbed a curtsy. "Lord David."

Lord David and Dr. Drinker regarded one another in obvious curiosity, so Cassandra introduced them.

"Beaufort? Haven't I heard of you?" Dr. Drinker asked.

Lord David raised an eyebrow. "Have you?"

"Yes, aren't you the nobleman who's been talking to businesses in the area? The filature and the tannery?"

"Ah." He glanced at Cassandra. Should she leave? "I suppose you have, then."

"What were you talking to businesses about?" Cassandra asked.

Lord David looked to her. She couldn't quite understand his expression, as if . . . as if he had something more he wished to say to her.

Oh, she doubted she wanted to hear any more of what he had to say. What would he do, attempt to put her in her place as his inferior again? Reveal what she'd done for him to ruin her?

Dr. Drinker would be the last person in the city to judge her for taking care of the ill, and yet Cassandra's stomach quailed.

"Business," Lord David finally told Dr. Drinker, although Cassandra had been the one to pose the question to him. His smile was affable enough that the one-word answer didn't seem dismissive.

Was this the Lord David she'd known? She watched him for a moment. He looked like the same man, the same striking blue eyes, straight nose and handsome face.

"Is that your purpose?" Cassandra asked. Somehow, after all the things they'd talked about, she'd hoped there would be more substance to his purpose. Businesses were fine— necessary, of course—but simply increasing his fortune hardly seemed as though it would have required him to leave England, his home.

"My purpose?" Lord David faltered for a moment. "I hope. I hear you've settled on yours?"

Cassandra glanced up at Dr. Drinker, her new tutor. "I have."

Lord David followed her gaze. "Ah. Wonderful."

"Did you know?" Dr. Drinker said. "Miss Crofton is quite extraordinary."

"Hm." He made it sound as though that really were an interesting tidbit.

"How do you know Miss Crofton?" Dr. Drinker asked.

Lord David hesitated a moment, not looking at her. "Ah, we're . . . old friends."

Were they?

"He's leased the apartment upstairs from my uncle," Cassandra said.

Dr. Drinker accepted her explanation, as did Lord David, albeit with more resignation. He turned to Cassandra. "Would you please tell your uncle I wish to speak with him in the morning?"

"Certainly."

Lord David bowed from the neck to each of them and took his leave.

Cassandra waited until the door upstairs closed before she addressed Dr. Drinker. "Whom did you hear about Lord David from?"

"Oh, a friend of mine is an overseer at the tannery. It seems your friend is after worthy colonial businesses that he can help."

"Is he?" Worthy colonial businesses? Perhaps he couldn't do that in England. But what exactly did that mean?

Dr. Drinker finally released her arm. "Tomorrow?"

"Yes, thank you."

He left, and Cassandra seated herself in the corner to watch the clerks prepare their final report. And not to watch the stairwell. At least not very much.

Chapter 13

Lord David pondered the bookcases in his study as if he had the time or inclination to read today.

What he really needed was a distraction. It had been nearly fourteen hours since he'd seen Cassandra, and, unfortunately, he'd been able to think of little else.

Dr. Adam Drinker. Who was this man? Cassandra looked to him for her purpose? After how Josiah had gone on and on about how proud he was of Cassandra's work with the poor and the ill? How long could she have known this Drinker? With a name like that, how could she be sure he was no drunkard?

Lord David shook off the notion. His thoughts had suddenly developed a terrible habit of transporting him to the ridiculous. The man's name did not mean he was a drunkard. Cassandra had better judgment than that, he hoped. She'd certainly given him wide berth when he had shown no respect to her, so he would hope Drinker would give her that much.

Lord David had certainly failed her.

But he was trying to do better. Even if it could never be enough to undo his words.

Westing opened the door to the study. "The coach is here, my lord."

"Thank you, Westing."

Today's meeting was particularly delicate. It had taken some doing to find a sea captain who was willing to talk to him, but after speaking with a number of merchants and businesses in town, he had begun to see how important trade by sea was within the colonies.

If there was something he could do to help other people in the colonies—people who needed support far more than any business he'd known in England—it was beginning to feel like his duty.

The last thing he needed today was to be distracted by Cassandra. She had found her path forward, and clearly it had nothing to do with him. He'd made that happen. He needed to accept that.

By the time the coach reached its destination, Lord David had nearly fully returned his focus to business. He had made the calculated decision to forgo a wig today, as no one he'd met with previously had worn one, and wear his plainest clothes, which were still a bit obvious in their value.

The coach pulled up in front of the warehouse, and Lord David climbed out and walked directly up to the door. The occupant answered quickly: a tall, broad man in a gray coat in the simpler homespun style of Philadelphians. The captain might have been his own age.

He could not have imagined meeting with a ship's captain to discuss business a month before, and yet, here he was. "Captain Carter?" he asked.

He offered his hand. "Are you to be my investor?"

"I hope so. Beaufort," Lord David introduced himself. His name without any title felt like an oddly fitting shoe.

"Come in," Carter invited him.

In the narrow confines of his office, Carter had laid out a map, with various shipping routes along the American coast marked in colored ink. "You're new to the colonies?"

"Very." Admitting as much humbled him, but perhaps that was for the best.

Surely Cassandra would think so.

Carter pointed out the routes on the map, identifying which goods were traded between colonies. The number was disappointing. "We do still depend heavily on imports from Britain," Carter concluded, "or our own raw materials being processed into finished goods over there and then sold back to us."

Carter's hand came to rest on Boston, one of the other main ports along the coast, in addition to Philadelphia and New York. The only thing Lord David knew of Boston was the engraving he'd seen in the tavern on his first day in the colonies. The Boston Massacre. British soldiers firing on defenseless colonists.

Small wonder men like Carter were becoming more interested in trade within the colonies.

Finally, the feeling he'd been waiting for all these weeks came: this was right. This was his purpose.

"All right," Lord David said. "What can I do?"

Cassandra found herself in another dim sickroom, but now it was without the quiet desperation and torment of the smallpox. She gave Dr. Drinker the correct fleam from his case. The hinged device concealed a number of triangular blades for opening a vein. Dr. Drinker was particularly conservative when it came to letting a patient, but for this elderly woman with a fever that would not abate, it seemed necessary.

Her official duties complete, Cassandra took the patient's other hand in hers and wet a rag to mop her brow. "Rest, Mrs. Gibson," she said. "You need to rest."

Mrs. Gibson sucked in air when the blade pierced her skin. She was already so pale that Cassandra was worried about her even without the fever.

She wet another rag and laid it on the woman's collarbones. Her breath was short and shallow.

Cassandra had already lost more patients than she'd ever wish to in Germantown, most of them children. That didn't make it any easier to watch someone who could have been her grandmother slipping from this life.

She barely remembered her grandmother, her mother's mother, and Uncle Josiah's. But something about this woman's wiry white hair brought her to mind again. She'd loved to read to Cassandra and Helen, until her eyesight failed.

Perhaps that was why Cassandra had thought of reading to Lord David.

How long had it been, and her thoughts still strayed to him? He had certainly cast her off discourteously, to misquote that old lay allegedly by Henry VIII. He hadn't seemed overly regretful the one time she'd seen him since. And that was fine with her. She'd never wanted to make his acquaintance in the first place.

Cassandra held on to Mrs. Gibson as her breathing slowed to a normal rate. Dr. Drinker allowed Cassandra to bind up the cut while he disposed of the blood. They watched the bandage, and her, for a long moment, to make sure all would be well.

As far as they could see, it would be. But a mere month of practicing "real" medicine had already taught her a dear lesson:

there were no guarantees and no way of seeing the future. This could well be Mrs. Gibson's final illness.

They assured Mrs. Gibson's daughter they had done all they could. "Keep the rags on her head and chest refreshed with cool liquid," Cassandra added. "For her comfort."

"Thank you for your kindness," the daughter said.

The words stirred a memory almost as old as that of her grandmother. They were the exact words she'd heard a dozen people say to her mother.

The daughter pressed a coin into Dr. Drinker's hand. Cassandra had also learned that they might well be owed the difference between that payment and their fee forever.

Medicine was a cruel business in many ways, but if he could escape starving, Dr. Drinker had vowed not to force that fate on a patient or their family.

"You know, you really are a comfort to everyone we see," Dr. Drinker said once they were outside. The sun was high once they left the Gibsons', but Cassandra's spirits were not.

"Thank you," she managed. She was beginning to see that comforting was an art she'd been tutored in far longer than medicine.

"Would you like to take dinner with your family?" he offered.

It was a good idea, she had to admit. They were much closer to her home than his, and Uncle Josiah had issued him a standing invitation to join them for meals. "Let's," she said on a sigh.

Transportation was one luxury a doctor could not do without, and Dr. Drinker's hooded carriage was small and light to help him attend emergencies better. Cassandra had no doubt but that riding with him probably looked scandalous, but she'd racked up a number of scandalous behaviors since she'd come to the colonies.

A fine way for a gentleman's daughter to behave.

She chuckled to herself. She was no longer sure that held any meaning. She would always be the daughter of Thomas Crofton, but what did his status matter to her life? She was making her own life here now, and she had something to contribute.

Besides, even if she were ruined in this society, she still knew hardly anyone aside from her family, the doctor and her German patients.

And Lord David. But who cared what he thought?

The drive back to her uncle's house was short, and Dr. Drinker handed her down from his little carriage. If she was not mistaken, he had begun taking her arm more often. He was a kind man, and he certainly did respect her and what she did. She could easily marry him and be completely happy.

Or completely not.

She did not object when he took her arm, however, and they walked into the house together.

It took a very long moment for Cassandra to understand the scene in the drawing room before her. Her sister and cousins were gathered about the room, Verity having apparently induced Mercy into playacting one of Constance's comedies before the fireplace. Verity wore a very fine man's coat, blue with silver scrolling embroidery. Even her aunt and uncle were laughing.

And there, in the middle of it all, laughing along with them, was . . . Lord David? Precisely as she'd seen him last: without a coat or wig. And perfectly at home.

How—why—when had he become part of her family?

He glanced over and saw her and Dr. Drinker at the door and instantly stood. His expression darkened.

Yes, that was him. He'd definitely recognized her.

Cassandra looked away from him as the room's attention

shifted to her. "Good afternoon. You all know Dr. Drinker?" She hoped they wouldn't have to go through a round of introductions.

Her cousins seemed more or less familiar with him, and she quickly introduced Helen.

Uncle Josiah came over to shake his hand. "So glad you could join us."

"We didn't realize you had other company," Cassandra said. "We can certainly eat elsewhere."

"Nonsense. Our home is always open."

Right on time, Polly appeared at the door to announce dinner. Lord David approached Verity first, and she shrugged out of his coat. Constance beat Temperance to claim his arm. Apparently something of the etiquette lessons Helen had been giving them had set in, because Temperance didn't help herself to his other arm. Cassandra and Helen were both fairly certain the standard etiquette for formal dining in country estates didn't quite apply in colonial city life, but it never hurt to learn.

As Dr. Drinker already had Cassandra's arm, he accompanied her to the dining room. She caught Helen's eye and the little show of excitement she conveyed, but she found she felt none of it herself.

She liked Dr. Drinker very much. Appreciated him even more. But that was all she felt for him.

She watched Lord David as he helped Constance to her seat. Dr. Drinker did her the same courtesy, seating her directly across from Lord David.

If Dr. Drinker had any designs on her hand, this seating arrangement of his was a very stupid idea.

Lord David met her gaze, and she quickly looked away. Why must he always act as though he had something to say to her? Surely he'd already said enough.

Polly and Ginny placed the first course on the table and

joined them. Roasted beef and Polly's best brown bread were normally Cassandra's favorite, but she found she had lost her appetite.

Aunt Anne leaned close. "Are you well, my dear?"

"Yes, thank you." She forced herself to take a bite of beef.

"Lord David," Uncle Josiah began, "how goes your business?"

"Oh, I'm sure no one wants to speak of such things at the table."

"And your purpose?" The words were out before Cassandra could stop them.

Lord David was stunned for a moment but met her eyes again. "I think I've found it, yes."

"Good." She very much wanted to know what that purpose was, and it would have been the next logical question to ask a friend. But they were not friends. Her gaze fell to her plate.

"And how is medicine, Doctor?" Lord David asked. "If we're talking business."

"It has its ups and downs," Dr. Drinker admitted. "But our downs are typically a bit different than in other lines of work."

The table grew somber a moment.

Dr. Drinker turned to Cassandra. "Wouldn't you say?"

"Indeed."

Lord David looked between Dr. Drinker and her. "Do you speak of medicine often? To one another?" he asked. He seemed . . . perplexed?

"Daily?" Cassandra replied. "I've found speaking is generally helpful when one is trying to teach another a trade."

Lord David blinked twice, then gave a little headshake. "Trying to do what?"

"Miss Crofton—Cassandra," Dr Drinker clarified, as there were two Miss Croftons present, "is studying medicine."

"From you?"

"No, from the Governor." Cassandra glanced at Temperance and added, "And his son."

Temperance beamed.

Uncle Josiah cleared his throat. Obviously he'd had enough of how she'd treated Lord David at his table. "Apologies," she murmured.

"Please don't apologize," Lord David said. "I've missed that."

What? Surely she hadn't heard him correctly. No one could have missed her sarcasm, least of all her favorite victim.

Lord David continued, speaking to Dr. Drinker. "I'm sure she has quite a talent."

"That she does."

Cassandra couldn't tell which one of them spoke with more pride in his voice. Why was Lord David being kind to her? Why was he here? Even her family hadn't expected her, and yet now he wasn't at all unhappy to see her?

It felt as though the floor—or simply the situation—was slowly tilting past her control or comprehension. Her stomach felt as though she were back on the boat again. What on earth was happening?

Aunt Anne touched her arm. Before she could ask after Cassandra's wellbeing again, Cassandra stood. "I . . . I need to rest." She addressed Dr. Drinker. "Take your time. Fetch me before you go, if you please."

"Certainly."

"Please excuse me," she bid the rest of the table, and she hurried out.

She was trying not to obviously flee the room, so she was not fast enough to escape the sound of another chair pushing back from the table. She had almost made the stairs when a hand grasped hers.

Cassandra shouldn't have been surprised to find Lord

David behind her, but she still was. She pulled free of his fingers and glanced up the stairs.

"I must speak with you," Lord David said.

The urgency in his voice and his sapphire eyes were the only thing that kept her from fleeing whatever harsh rebuke she might have anticipated.

Her gaze dropped to the floor. "I'm sorry, that was rude of me."

"What?"

"The governor." She gestured back at the dining room as if he needed the reminder.

"As I said, I miss your wit."

"You don't miss being its victim, to be sure."

Lord David's expression agreed to that concession. "I might prefer it aimed in another direction." He glanced over his shoulder. At the door to the dining room, two heads popped out of sight.

Lord David scanned the drawing room, but nowhere afforded them more privacy. "Can we sit? Can I ... talk to you?"

"We've already said enough, haven't we?"

His mouth worked in silence for a moment before he closed it. "Have we?" he finally asked.

"I've nothing more to say."

"And I've said too much." Lord David looked away from her, his grimace betraying ... pain?

Why should *he* feel any pain, simply because he'd injured her?

He began to turn away, and Cassandra's heart caught in her chest as much as it had that day when he'd dismissed her. "We can sit," she said quickly.

She couldn't tell whether Lord David was more surprised or relieved, but he led her back to the pink velvet couch, where they settled at either end.

Another glance at the door sent two little spies scuttling away again. The sounds of Uncle Josiah's gentle reprimand carried from the other room.

Lord David sat across the couch from her, his gaze intense upon her.

What on earth did he have to say?

Chapter 14

"Cassandra," Lord David began. "May—may I call you that?"

"For the moment."

He was fortunate to receive even provisional permission. He cleared his throat. Why would the words not come?

How difficult was it to say *I'm sorry?*

He stared into her amber brown eyes, but no words followed.

After a long, awkward moment, Cassandra broke the silence. "Why are you here?"

"Your uncle invited me. I didn't know you'd be here."

"Ah. Sorry to disappoint."

"Not at all." He'd actually hoped to find her here. To have this very conversation. That he was failing at.

The conversation, such as it was, lapsed until Cassandra made another attempt. "You said you found your purpose?"

"Ah, yes."

"Would you . . . care to impart that purpose?"

She wanted to know? "Certainly. I've learned that the

colonies send most of their raw goods like cotton or wool to England, which sends back finished goods such as fabric. That seems terribly inefficient and unwise, so I'm going to be helping businesses that will make the colonies more economically independent."

Cassandra tilted her head quizzically. Had he not explained it well? "I didn't realize you'd put such depth into your business study."

"I've had excellent tutors."

"Ah, yes, that makes all the difference. Dr. Drinker has taught me so much."

He'd begun to suspect that Cassandra and the doctor were not courting, but that was the final confirmation he wanted. He resettled himself on the couch, moving a little closer so he could lower his voice. "You were already a very talented nurse."

"Apparently not." Her tone was clipped.

And that was his fault. Guilt stabbed like a dagger in his chest. "Cassandra, I am so sorry. I shouldn't have thrown you out. I regret it every day."

"It was an abominable way to treat your oldest friend."

He couldn't help a smile. Was it too much to hope that was still true? "And I'm so very sorry for it."

Cassandra was quiet for a long moment. "Why would you treat me so?"

The pain in her voice flayed his heart again, but he had to tell her the truth, awful as it was. "I thought I saw ... pity in your eyes. Contempt."

Her eyebrows knitted together, and Lord David pressed on. "I was wrong to show you so little courtesy. Respect. I—so many other people in my life have treated *me* that way, and I thought—I couldn't bear to have a country gentleman's daughter scorn me."

"Oh." The syllable carried a little descending note of disappointment.

"But I was wrong there, too." The thoughts that had been spinning in his mind the last few weeks were finally starting to coalesce around an idea that would have upended his life a month ago, let alone three. "I'm beginning to see that—that's the wrong thing to be concerned about. Rank, birth, they mean virtually nothing here. The smallpox didn't care a fig if I were King George himself. What matters is what we do. The difference we choose to make."

Cassandra shifted on the couch—closer?—as she pondered his words. "Yes. That's precisely what I've been thinking. That's what I love about nursing: helping others."

"That's your purpose."

She nodded.

That was why she'd looked at the doctor when he'd asked about her purpose at the office. "I was wondering how a gentleman's daughter got to be so good at nursing."

Cassandra's smile was small, but it brightened her countenance more than the sun did the sky. "I'm more than that, you know. I'm a kind woman's daughter."

Lord David reached for her hand. "You are indeed."

She looked down at his hand and back up at him.

"Please don't ever leave me," he said, staring into her amber eyes.

"Lord David—"

"No."

Cassandra gave him another quizzical expression. Apparently he was being difficult, though he wasn't trying to be. "I—I can't use my title any longer."

"Did your father say something?"

"Oh, no." He waved a hand. "He probably still hasn't noticed I've left. I simply want to stay here, with people I care about."

"And what of your title?"

"Here, it means virtually nothing," he said.

Cassandra laughed a moment, and it sounded like the same wonder he felt. This was the last thing he'd expected to find when he'd come to the colonies to prove himself, to find that he'd never needed proof in the first place. He merely needed meaningful work and to be far away from his family.

His courtesy title was the last thing tying him to that entire system. He would be glad to hear it gone.

"I think I know the answer," he said, "but to be certain— Dr. Drinker is not courting you, is he?"

"No, though he might mean to." Cassandra's smile bore a trace of pain in sympathy. The very look he'd mistaken for pity and scorn was just another manifestation of her kindness.

"He'll have to wait his turn." He braced himself. "*If* your oldest friend in the colonies might … be welcome to try his hand?"

Cassandra beamed at him. "I shall have to let the doctor know gently."

On an impulse—that he'd been fighting for longer than he should admit—he leaned forward and kissed her quickly, as if that sealed the agreement of the beginning of their courtship.

Giggling behind them cut short any other display of affection, and when he pulled back, he saw Cassandra's blush. "Oh, I'm sorry, I hope I haven't ruined you to your family."

"I don't know, but it certainly wouldn't be the first time."

"I'll go back for appearances. You can take your rest." He began to stand.

She kept hold of his hand. "I'm feeling much better."

"Good." He started for the dining room again, but Cassandra did not follow, pulling him to a stop.

"Wait a moment. What shall I call you now?"

"Oh, His Majestic Worshipfulness Lord Popinjay of Coxcomb, naturally."

Cassandra laughed. "Yes, Your Magnificence." She used his help to regain her feet as well and treated him with a smile that clearly conveyed she was waiting for her real answer.

"David," he said. "Simply David."

"Certainly, David," she said. And it sounded perfect on her lips.

So he kissed them again, and this time he didn't let any giggling deter him.

Epilogue

Helen sat alone in the corner of her aunt's drawing room, watching the party. Her new brother-in-law made his way around the room, heartily thanking the guests for coming as if they were his own kith and kin.

She assumed most of the guests were friends of her aunt or clients of her uncle who could not resist the opportunity to gawk at a scion of English nobility. Certainly neither David nor she and Cassandra could boast so many acquaintances in the colonies. If Cassandra had married at Heartcomb, they would have had scores of their own friends to invite.

Helen pushed the thought of Heartcomb out of her mind. Dwelling on the past did no good, and she had plenty to worry her about the future. Cassandra would live in David's home now, and Helen would be left alone with her cousins. She couldn't begrudge her sister her happiness, but Helen had already made an unsupportable number of changes in such a brief stretch of time.

How could she bear to lose the last member of her family?

Temperance grabbed Helen's arm, startling her into nearly

falling off her chair.

"He's here!" Temperance bounced on her toes, nearly beside herself with excitement. "I'd hoped he would come!"

Helen did not need to look up to confirm whom Temperance spoke of, though she did anyway. Temperance's obsession with Winthrop Morley, son of the Governor of Pennsylvania, must have been renowned all the way to New England. She talked of nothing else to every single person she met. Helen had to admit to herself that she was curious to compare the fantasy of the man to his actual person.

The sight of him startled her more than Temperance had. He was young, perhaps early twenties, and his manner of dress surely would rival the most elegant suit of clothes the King of England could command. Even David, dressed in a ruby red coat trimmed with coordinating silk and velvet, was eclipsed by Winthrop's floral brocade coat with ribbon, rope, and embroidered W's. Could this be real? Helen had to blink to make sure she hadn't accidentally fallen asleep.

Winthrop turned and caught sight of Temperance, then proceeded to mince over to them in heels of at least four inches height. They were balanced by a four-inch-high white wig atop his head.

"Mister Morley," Temperance sighed, extending her hand to him.

He bowed nearly to the ground and then took her hand. Was that supposed to be a handshake, or did he expect her to kiss his ring? "Miss Hayes."

Temperance stared at Winthrop adoringly. Helen thought she might be sick.

Winthrop turned to her. "And who is this?"

Helen pasted on an insincere smile as Temperance reluctantly introduced her to Winthrop.

"Come and refresh yourself." Temperance took his arm

and steered him toward the food.

Helen chuckled a little. Temperance was making light work of proving her affection to Winthrop.

David watched Temperance and Winthrop strut past as he reached Helen's corner. "There you are. We haven't seen you since we left the church, sister."

She'd never been addressed that way before by a man—or anyone other than Cassandra. "David."

He was still staring after Winthrop, barely concealing a laugh. "I don't know whether to be more offended he's shown up me or my wife."

"I'll tell her you think so."

"Don't be ridiculous. Look at my wife: she's radiant."

He was right. Cassandra's new crimson damask silk *robe à la française* was only outshone by her smile.

A high-pitched guffaw pealed over the jovial crowd. Helen was scarcely surprised to trace the cackle to Winthrop Macaroni—rather, Morley.

"How *does* he wear a wig that tall?" David mused.

"And those heels?" Helen laughed with him.

David took a sip of his punch and grimaced, eyeing his mug. "Is this what we've been serving all night?"

"I believe so." She hadn't tried it.

"Dreadful." He set the mug on the nearest side table.

She resisted the urge to snort. He might have left off using his courtesy title, but underneath, was he still the same pompous nobleman they'd met on the ship from England nine months ago? What had her sister gotten herself into, going off with this man?

David turned to Helen. "Do you mean to speak to my wife at some point tonight?"

"You quite like calling her 'my wife,' don't you?"

He grinned. "Am I that obvious?"

Helen nodded, glad he'd taken the bait of the subject change. He was right there, too, though. She should go speak to her sister, but she couldn't quite manage it. Every time she thought about what to say a lump the size of a grapefruit rose up in her throat.

"Captain Carter," David called. "You came!"

A tall man dressed in unrelieved black strode purposefully toward them.

"May I introduce you?" David asked Helen before the other man arrived.

"I suppose." She accepted his offered hand to help her to her feet.

The man in black reached them, and David began the introduction. "Helen, may I present Captain—sorry, what's your given name?"

The man furrowed his brow. "Nathaniel."

"Ah. Captain Nathaniel Carter. Carter, this is Miss Helen Crofton, my new sister."

Another new title he kept repeating. "Pleased to meet you," Helen said politely.

Captain Carter nodded curtly and turned back to David. "I have that information you requested."

He'd barely acknowledged her. What shocking rudeness.

David clapped him on the back. "I'm sure that can wait. It's my wedding day! Come, have some punch." He glanced at his abandoned mug. "Or something else."

Helen rolled her eyes at their retreating backs. Good riddance to Captain Taciturn.

"Cousin, would you like some cake?" Verity Hayes approached, offering Helen a plate. "I helped to make it."

"Thank you." Helen accepted the cake. She would need something to bolster her courage to speak to Cassandra, and cake was likely the strongest thing they had.

She took a bite, and the overpowering flavor of nutmeg seized her mouth. She tried not to gag. She didn't want to offend her cousin by spitting out the whole mouthful, but it was difficult to swallow without chewing further. Unfortunately, the cake did not seem to yield to chewing. Had they dropped a pebble in the batter?

Her teeth made a loud crunch on the pebble, and her cousin turned back to her. "You've found it!" Verity exclaimed. "You got the nutmeg."

Everyone who'd eaten this cake must have gotten plenty of nutmeg. Helen again tried to swallow, but the pebble threatened to lodge itself in her throat. A mug was thrust in her face and she drank deeply, grateful to clear her throat.

Perhaps it was the aftereffects of so much spice, but she had to agree with David. This punch was weak and honestly terrible.

"Thank you," she rasped. She looked up to see who had saved her and found Captain Carter. He scrutinized her as if she were a horse he wasn't sure about buying.

She couldn't help a little cough. To her complete horror, Captain Carter thumped her hard on the back. A tiny wad of cake flew from her mouth.

Mortified, Helen flew forward to retrieve the crumb, knocking over the empty punch cup.

"You shall be the next to marry!" Verity announced.

Helen looked uncomprehendingly from Verity to Captain Carter. Was this some kind of punishment in the colonies? Spew one's cake and one was forced to marry the man who tried to dislodge it?

Aunt Anne rushed over to them when she noticed Helen on her hands and knees, frozen in humiliation.

Captain Carter slid a hand under her elbow and helped her to stand.

"Thank you," Helen muttered, cupping the chewed cake in one hand. Hopefully nobody would notice when she threw it in the fire.

"She got the nutmeg, Mama," Verity informed her mother.

"Oh dear, we should have warned you! It is a tradition here in the colonies. One nutmeg is left whole in the bride's cake, and the person who finds it is next of all the guests to marry."

"I see," Helen said. Perhaps they could make a joke of it. "I thought—" She broke off and stared at Captain Carter, who was not smiling. "Never mind."

Captain Carter stooped to pick up the discarded mug and shoved it at her. Helen accepted it and dropped the crumb inside. It clinked against the metal. Ah, the nutmeg.

No more cake or punch for her.

Captain Carter glanced behind himself and then stepped aside to reveal Cassandra. "Sister dear, what happened? Why were you on the floor?"

"Oh, I'm fine." And hopefully Captain Carter would take the cue to end their awkward conversation and go away.

He simply stood there.

She attempted to focus on her sister, who was still positively glowing. Then pain creased Cassandra's features. "We're leaving."

Helen caught a little gasp. The moment she opened her mouth, she would start to cry.

They had never lived apart before.

Cassandra's chin trembled, and she drew Helen in for a hug.

"I'm not going far," Cassandra murmured.

Helen stifled a sob. She found she couldn't speak above a whisper either. "I don't know what I'll do without you."

Cassandra held her at arm's length, her eyes full of tears. Her husband appeared at her side. "What's this, dearest?"

David sounded mildly terrified.

Helen had always been the one to call Cassandra "dearest." That was all it took to break the dam holding back Helen's tears, and that set Cassandra off as well.

David looked from his wife to Helen. "We can't have tears on our wedding day!"

Helen turned to dab her cheeks surreptitiously. She inadvertently made eye contact with Captain Carter, who was staring at her with horror. Really? He was going to stand there and gape at their pain? Helen had never encountered such an ill-mannered man in her life! She hoped never to have to see him after today.

"We've never been separated," Cassandra was explaining to David. "Never fear; we shall rally."

David frowned. "Nonsense! I could never sacrifice your happiness for mine! Helen, you must make your home with us."

Helen turned to Cassandra, who was just as surprised as she was.

"What?" David consulted each of them. "No?"

"Are you certain?" Cassandra asked him.

"To be sure." David already had an arm around Cassandra's waist, but he pulled Helen in to join in an embrace. "My wife and my new sister under the same roof. What could be better?"

"What do you say, Helen?" Cassandra asked. "Maybe you had rather stay here."

"If you'll have me, I'd love to come," Helen assured her.

"Wonderful!" David said. "Bring out more punch! Or do you have anything else?"

Helen smiled. Some things might never change about her new brother, but he had his good points. She threw her arms around David and Cassandra. Perhaps her family wasn't shrinking after all.

Dear Reader,

Thank you so much for reading *A Gentleman's Daughter*! I'm excited to share my first sweet historical romance with you. I hope you'll continue to join us for all the romance of the Revolution!

Do you know the best way to thank an author when you enjoy a book? We do love getting notes from happy readers, but even more helpful is leaving a review online on Amazon or Goodreads. Reviews also help writers get advertising spots and spread the word about a book.

Until my next book comes out, I'd like to invite you to join my mailing group! I've got lots of fun bonuses there, like pictures of the clothing inspiration and Lord David's coat of arms. Join me here: http://love.didavisauthor.com/newsletter1

Thanks again for reading, and I hope to see you again soon!

Love,

Diana Davis

Acknowledgements

As with all of my books, telling this story was only possible with lots of help! My first thanks must go to my family, who are patient and supportive of my writing. So thank you to my husband, children, parents, siblings, and best friend of over twenty years for always supporting my job/hobby/habit/obsession!

I want to give many thanks to my collaborator Audrey Glenn and my beta readers, author Donna K. Weaver, Susan Turner, Diana Franklin, and author Ranée S. Clark, who all gave extremely helpful feedback and encouragement. Thank you!

Thanks once again to Sally Johnson, my proofreader, coworker and cheerleader!

I'm grateful to God for giving me this gift, a passion for writing, for reminding me not to hide it under a bushel, and for putting the people that I need most in my path (even if it takes me a while to recognize them sometimes).

And I'm grateful to you, reader, for joining me!

About the Author

Diana Davis was born and raised in North Carolina. She is also the author of the Dusky Cove cozy mystery series. She has been writing fiction with Audrey Glenn since they were teenagers, and they share an interest in history.

Diana holds a Bachelor degree in American Studies and taught a course on constitutional history as an undergraduate teaching assistant. She is a candidate for the Master of Fine Art from Vermont College of Fine Arts. She makes her home in the Rocky Mountains with her husband and children.

Diana loves to hear from readers! You can reach her at didavisauthor@gmail.com.

Printed in Great Britain
by Amazon